Uprooted

A Lily Deene Novel

Annie Grace Roberts

Uprooted
A Lily Deene Novel #3

ISBN: (ebook) 978-1-953335-86-9
(print) 978-1-953335-93-7

Inkspell Publishing
207 Moonglow Circle #101
Murrells Inlet, SC 29576

Cover art by: Fantasia Frog Designs
Edited by: Yezanira Venecia

DEDICATION

For Chook, who fought in WW2

Wait for me and I'll return, defying every death.
And let those who do not wait say that I was lucky.
They will never understand that in the midst of death
You with your waiting saved me.
Only you and I will know how I survived:
It was because you waited as no one else did.

Konstantin Simonov. (1915-1979)

PROLOGUE

Alderney Island
Prisoner of War Camp
1943
Spring

Heinrich had traveled from Germany with a group of young soldiers in the back of a military truck. They rode for hours in the cold, sitting on hard wooden benches.

"We are in France," their driver had announced after they crossed some invisible boundary. "You have twenty minutes to stretch your legs and piss."

Heinrich and the other soldiers, stiff from sitting so long, had scrambled out of the back like young schoolboys on an outing, full of good spirits, anxious to get their first look at Nazi-occupied France. To Heinrich's disappointment, there hadn't been much to see. Snow-covered fields bordered the road. In the distance, a small stone farmhouse and a barn huddled together in the winter landscape. An old man, most likely the farmer, had stood mending a fence across the road from where they had stopped. He'd looked up briefly, his eyes wary and suspicious, but said nothing and soon returned to his task.

After taking care of business, Heinrich joined the other soldiers huddled around the truck. A few smoked cigarettes, most just stood hunched in the cold, stamping their feet as their warm breath created puffs of mist in the cold, winter air. Their driver, a short square man with a brutish flat face, shouted something to the farmer. The farmer did not reply.

The driver shouted a second time. Again, the farmer ignored him. Red-faced and angry, their driver marched across the road.

Heinrich watched with interest. He remembered puffing out his chest indignantly at the French farmer's lack of respect for them. After all, it was Occupied France. That part of France was German territory. Even if the farmer didn't understand German, he should have made an effort. Nazi soldiers should be shown respect.

"Who does that peasant farmer think he is?" one of the other soldiers had commented.

"It looks like our driver is going to teach the *Franzmann* some manners," another said. They all laughed.

The loud crack of a pistol shot caused Heinrich to flinch in shocked surprise. He'd watched as the driver calmly holstered his pistol before bending over to search the dead farmer's pockets. Blood leached onto the snow, staining it crimson. The driver removed the farmer's leather boots before turning toward Heinrich and the rest of the soldiers, gesturing for them to get into the truck.

They'd climbed into the back, no longer laughing.

It had been more than a year ago, but Heinrich could still recall the color of the dead farmer's socks. He had enlisted to prove his loyalty to the Fatherland, and if he was honest with himself, to be a great hero. It all seemed so childish now. War wasn't cheering crowds, parades, and shiny medals; it was people dying miserable deaths, starved, beaten, frozen, skin scorched black by fire, limbs severed, guts spilling out of them. He had seen it all and it sickened him. This war was changing him into someone he did not want to be. Changing him into someone he didn't think he could live with.

CHAPTER 1

LILY

December 7
10:00 a.m.

Something was wrong with me. My head ached and throbbed. My mouth was dry. I tried to lick my lips, but my tongue felt abnormally thick and heavy in my mouth and I couldn't quite manage it.

I opened my eyes cautiously, feeling confused and disoriented. The dark was so complete that for a moment I wasn't sure if I was awake or dreaming? I blinked. I blinked again and I slowly became aware of sensations. Cold. I was very cold.

I struggled to sit up. My arms and legs felt like stone weights. I managed to lift myself a little, but my stomach heaved, and I had to lie down quickly to keep from throwing up.

What was wrong with me? I breathed deeply, drinking in the cold and dark in large gulping breaths as I tried to snag the half-formed thoughts that floated past like drifting clouds. Why was it so dark? Was I sick? Where was my pillow? My comforter? Where was I?

Gingerly, I moved my fingers testing the area around me. I lay on a hard surface, stone or brick. I wasn't in my bed. I should have been in my bed. My head swam with the effort as I tried to figure out what was happening to me. My mind was in a fog. I had no recollection of coming to this place.

Again, I tried to sit up, and this time I managed to raise myself up on my elbows before I felt a sudden saltiness in the back of my throat. Once more, my stomach heaved and roiled. I quickly rolled over and retched, the hot sour smell of vomit permeating the air, worsening my nausea. I lay on my back, too dizzy and disoriented to move. Closing my eyes, I surrendered to the darkness.

CHAPTER 2

SIMON

December 6

After their phone call, he sent Lily a quick cheerful message about visiting her in London this weekend. He didn't expect to hear from her until later, so he wasn't worried when Lily didn't reply right away. Sometimes she turned off her mobile when she was studying.

He drove out to John Barlow's farm, where he spent a wet, cold afternoon wrestling worm-infested sheep into a muddy pen. She still hadn't rung him by the time he'd taken care of the last of the lot. He was mildly disappointed. He hoped she wasn't putting him off. *No*, he told himself. She would have told him straight away if she hadn't wanted him to visit. Most likely, she was hunched over her laptop working like a fiend on her paper. She'd ring him later tonight after she'd finished.

On the drive home, fat raindrops splattered the window of his car as the sky darkened overhead.

Distracted by his own thoughts, he didn't see the lumber in the road until it was too late. He managed to swerve around the larger pieces, but he couldn't avoid all of them. There was a loud *thump* as he ran over one of the splintered boards. He pulled to the side of the road and got out to inspect the damage. Bugger all! The last thing he wanted to do tonight was change out a punctured tire in the pouring rain.

By the time he got home, he was wet, cold, dirty, and in a foul mood. He let himself into the front door of his flat only to find his flatmates, Nigel and Audrey, curled up on the sofa.

He gave them a curt nod.

"What have you got up to?" Audrey asked him, eyeing his mud-spattered clothes.

"I had a puncture," Simon said, stripping off his mac.

"Poor bugger," Nigel commented. "You look like you could do with a pint."

"I could do with ten."

Audrey eyed him. "Why don't you come to the local with us tonight?"

Simon shook his head. "Thanks, but you don't need me joining your Friday night."

"C'mon, mate, it's us. We don't mind. Do we?" Nigel glanced over at Audrey.

"Not a bit. Besides," she added sympathetically, "you really do look like you could use a pint."

Simon checked his phone. Seven p.m. and still no message from Lily. Why not go to the pub? It certainly didn't look like he was going to be driving to London tonight anyway. "I've got to clean up a bit first," he said. "I'll meet you."

The usual Friday night crowd filled the pub. A group of old men, unhappy with the crush of young people taking over the pub, eyed him warily as they huddled over their drinks at the bar. He nodded to them and ordered his ale.

"Simon Fitzgibbon!"

He heard his name called and turned around. A short brunette was determinedly making her way through the crowd like a homing missile.

Simon sighed. The last thing he wanted to deal with tonight was Audrey's friend Carolyn. He gave her a quick nod before turning to grab his glass from the bar.

He pasted a smile on his face and turned around to face her.

"Hullo, Caro."

"Why didn't you tell me that you were coming tonight?" Carolyn accused him, one hand resting flirtatiously on a cocked hip.

"I didn't know I was." He scanned the crowd, catching sight of Nigel and Audrey by the billiards table. He nodded in Nigel's direction. "Nigel and Audrey talked me into it."

Carolyn looked over at them. "Just Nigel and Audrey?" She smiled up at him expectantly.

"Yeah."

Her face lit up. "I came here with Libby, but she's found herself a bloke. Why don't I join you and we can make it a double? Nigel and Audrey won't mind." Before Simon had a chance to say anything, Carolyn deftly tucked her arm into his and tugged him away from the bar.

"Come on then," she said, pulling him through the crowd. "Before someone else gets those seats."

"Hullo, you two." Carolyn greeted Nigel and Audrey as she pulled up a chair at the table. Nigel acknowledged Carolyn's addition to their party with a lift of an eyebrow in Simon's direction. Simon gave him a rueful shrug.

Audrey and Carolyn started chatting right away, while he and Nigel sipped their beers and waited for the band to begin playing. As the night wore on, Simon found himself drinking too much and flirting too much. He knew he was treading on dangerous ground, but he was feeling a bit sorry for himself. Not to mention a bit cheesed off that

Lily still hadn't rung him. Carolyn cozied up to him until she somehow ended up sitting on his lap with a self-satisfied smile.

He was finishing his third or maybe it was his fourth pint, when his mobile vibrated. He tried to fish it out of his back pocket without toppling Carolyn onto the floor.

"What are you doing?"

"I've a message. Move over a bit."

Carolyn slid off his lap. "Who is it?" she asked as he read the text message.

"A mate in London. I told him I'd pop round this weekend when I was at Lily's," Simon replied distractedly as he typed his reply.

Carolyn jumped angrily to her feet. "You're seeing Lily this weekend?"

Simon flinched, guiltily.

"What was all this about then? Just passing the time until you can see her?" She glared at him.

Simon opened his mouth, but realizing there was nothing he could say, closed it again.

"That's it, isn't it?" Tears filled her eyes. "You are such a bloody git, Simon!"

"Caro, I didn't mean …"

"Don't you dare say it! Don't you dare say it, Simon Fitzgibbon!" Her voice rose. She angrily spun around and pushed her way through the crowd.

Audrey fixed him with a withering look as Carolyn made her way to the front door. "She's right, you know," she said before standing up and following Carolyn.

Simon watched them feeling terrible. He hadn't meant to be cruel. He just hadn't been thinking.

"Not your best move, mate," Nigel commented.

"I'll go talk to her."

He shook his head. "Not a good idea. When Audrey and Caro get together and start bashing men, it's best to clear out."

Simon sighed heavily. "You're probably right." He

finished his ale quickly. “I’m off then.”

Nigel glanced at his mobile. “I expect I won’t see Audrey for a while.”

“Not much of a Friday night for you. Sorry about that.”

Nigel shrugged. “Audrey’ll come around. Besides,” he said with a toothy grin, “I should probably thank you.”

“Thank me?”

“Audrey’s always going on about how I don’t treat her right. Always talking about how wonderful you are.” He rolled his eyes, mimicking her with an unnaturally high voice, “‘Simon is so considerate. Why can’t you be more like Simon?’” He paused reverting to his natural speaking voice. “But after tonight, you’ve made me look like Prince Charming.”

“Thanks. Now I do feel like a proper tosser.”

“I believe the term was bloody tosser, or was it, proper git? I forget,” Nigel said, giving Simon a hearty slap on the back and laughing.

Simon left the pub and walked slowly back to his flat. The earlier rain had given way to a heavy wet fog. He thrust his hands in the pockets of his mac, hunching his shoulders against the cold and damp as he walked through the dark streets.

He had acted like a jealous schoolboy, chatting up Carolyn when he knew she fancied him, and for what? To show Lily that he didn’t need her? To prove to himself that he didn’t need Lily? He shook his head in disgust. Caro was right. He was a proper idiot.

Simon let himself into the flat feeling dispirited. To make himself feel better, he sent Lily a message asking how she was getting on with her paper. He waited a few minutes, eyeing his phone hopefully. No response.

He sighed, combing his fingers through his hair. It hadn’t gone eleven yet, but given the lack of options, he decided to put an end to a very bad day. He undressed and crawled into bed.

He woke just after midnight feeling that something was off. Too many pints, he thought, or maybe it was his guilty conscience pricking him. Groggily, he reached for his mobile and checked his messages. His heart lifted when he saw that Lily had finally responded to him while he was sleeping: *Finished my paper! Can't wait to see you tomorrow! Not too early.* He placed his phone on the night table and lay back, resting his head on his pillow, a smile of contentment on his face. His weekend was looking a great deal more promising.

CHAPTER 3

LILY MEETS HARRY

December 7
3:00 p.m.

"*Mach dir keine sorgen. Du bist hier sicher.*"

My heart slammed into my chest. There was someone here with me!

I held my breath. Willing myself to keep silent. I wanted to run and hide, but I was too terrified and confused to move. I sat in the cold and dark, shaking like a small, frightened animal. Hardly daring to breathe.

Silence surrounded me. Had I imagined that voice? I strained my ears, listening intently. Nothing. It must have been my imagination. I inhaled deeply, filling my lungs with frigid air, and let out a shaky breath.

"*Du bist hier sicher.*"

There was someone in here with me! Why wasn't he speaking English? I said nothing. I couldn't. My heart was pounding so hard against my ribs that I could hardly breathe.

He must have sensed my terror. Perhaps he heard the sound of my panicked breathing.

"*Du bist hier sicher,*" he repeated, his voice calm and soothing.

"Who are you? W-w-where am I?" I finally managed to stutter, fear squeezing my voice and turning it into a creaking whisper.

There was a moment's silence before he replied. "English. You speak English," he said slowly, choosing his words carefully. "Of course. Forgive me. It has been a long time." He paused. "Do not be afraid."

I was shivering uncontrollably now. "Where am I?" I squeaked.

"You are safe."

"But where am I? Who are you? Why am I here?"

He paused for a moment, as if he was thinking. "England," he said finally. "You are in London, England."

I inhaled deeply, fighting against the nausea, headache, and fear. How did I get here?" I tried again, my voice catching. "I was in my room. I was sleeping. I don't understand. I want to know where I am. How did I get here?"

"You are American." He sounded surprised.

"How did I get here?" I asked. "Who are you? Why am I here?" I repeated. "I don't understand what is happening to me!"

"A man brought you here."

"A man? Who? Why?"

"I do not know."

"Please, tell me what is going on? I don't understand what's happening to me!"

"I know you are afraid, but you must be strong." He spoke quietly but with a calm assurance.

"Who are you?" Panic was bubbling up inside of me. "Please tell me what is happening to me. Please!" Tears squeezed from my eyes.

Shhh," he soothed softly. "You must be quiet now. He is coming."

My throat closed. "Who?" I creaked.

"One man. He comes."

I broke out in a cold prickling sweat, my heart pounding once again in terrified anticipation. There was nowhere to go, nowhere to hide. I sat shaking and holding my breath as I listened and waited, the sound of my own panicked breathing echoing loudly in my ears.

I heard the faint sound of footsteps from somewhere in the dark. They stopped. There was a *thud*, as if something heavy had been dropped on the floor, then the sound of a lock clicking open. A shaft of light cut through the darkness like a knife, and a man appeared. He crouched in the doorway for a moment, his eyes staring at me through the slits of the ski mask covering his face. Half-moaning, half-sobbing in fear, I scuttled backward into the safety of the darkness. With a grunt, he pushed a small ice chest into the room, then quickly shut and locked the door, once again leaving the room in total darkness.

My heart felt like it was going to leap through my chest. I waited, shivering and panting.

"He is not here. You are safe."

"Who was that man?" I asked, fear making my voice shrill. "Who are you?"

"That man. I do not know who he is. My name is Harry. Do not be afraid."

"I don't understand. Where are we! Why are we here!"

"Shhh," he soothed. "You are safe. I am here. Do not be afraid."

"What is happening to me!"

"This man and another man, they carried you here. They leave you here and lock the door."

"Why? Why would someone do that to me?"

"I do not know."

I tried to wrap my head around what was happening to me. Someone had taken me from my room in the middle of the night and brought me here. Why?

"I don't understand what is going on." My throat felt tight and hot. "Do you think they want money?"

"Money?"

"A ransom. Do you think they want someone to pay them to let me go?"

"It is possible, but I do not know."

My thoughts flashed to Sir Richard, my stepfather. He had money. A lot of money. Had someone kidnapped me to make Sir Richard pay a ransom?

"Oh God," I said shakily. "Oh God! I've been kidnapped!"

The word kidnapped reverberated in my head as the darkness pressed in on me, suffocating me. Panic frothed up in the back of my throat, making me feel sick again. I leaned over, gagging and retching.

When I was done, I felt a little calmer. The fear was still there, but the panic was gone, as if I had emptied it out of me.

"You have to help me," I pleaded with Harry. "You have to help me get out of here!"

"I will help."

"How do I get out of here? I need to get out of here!"

"I do not know."

I didn't know who Harry was, but it didn't matter anymore. All that mattered was that I wasn't alone. "Where are you?" I asked, rocking to my knees.

"I am not certain."

"Where? Tell me where I can find you." I turned my head like an antenna trying to get a fix on the direction of his voice as I groped blindly in the darkness. His voice came from everywhere and nowhere.

"Where?" I demanded, desperation making my voice unnaturally loud. I swayed unsteadily on all fours, feeling dizzy and sick, as if I was falling into a deep abyss. I needed physical contact, something solid to hold onto to keep me from disappearing into the empty blackness that threatened to swallow me whole. "Where are you, Harry?"

"I will help you. You must be strong."

"Where are you? Tell me where you are!"

"I do not know."

My mind was still fuzzy. I shook my head trying to clear it and another wave of nausea surged through me. I was physically sick again. Then, too tired and despondent to care, I lay down on the cold brick floor. No longer able to keep the tears from falling, I curled into a ball and wept as I tried to piece together what had happened to me.

CHAPTER 4

ONE DAY EARLIER

December 6
1:00 p.m.

I fought my way through the throng of London's holiday shoppers as I exited the underground, lugging an umbrella, three shopping bags, and a purse. My cell phone rang. It took a lot of juggling, but I managed to answer it before the call went to voicemail. It was Simon.

"Hey," I said into the phone, happiness in my voice. Someone jostled my elbow as they rushed past me. "Hang on a minute."

I cradled the phone in my neck temporarily, tucked my umbrella under my arm, and with some grunting and a great deal of effort, I managed to switch all three shopping bags to my other hand. "Okay. I'm back," I said, holding the phone with a free hand, panting slightly.

"What was that then? You sound as if you've been wrestling sheep, which is what I will be doing this afternoon."

"No sheep here," I told him, laughing. "I'm just trying to hold on to my bags."

"You've been shopping? What for?"

"Christmas! Of course! I don't want to show up at Brynmoor without any Christmas presents."

"Did you buy something for me?"

"Maybe. Maybe not."

"Hmm. I thought you were supposed to be writing a paper. You've finished already?"

"Not exactly," I hedged. "But I've made a good start on it." Which was more or less true. I mean, technically I had started it. True, I hadn't gotten very far, but I always work better under pressure anyway.

"Besides," I told him, "I had to go shopping today. Marks and Spencer was having a sale."

"A sale? That's your excuse for skiving off?"

"It was a very big sale."

"Right."

The heavy gray mist was beginning to turn into a light rain. Umbrellas snapped open as people hurried to find their cars or their homes before it really began raining. I thought briefly about unfurling my umbrella, but then I would have to hang up. Talking with Simon was definitely worth the risk of getting a little wet.

"No, really. The sale ended today. I had no choice. I had to go shopping. Besides, the term doesn't end for another week—I have enough time to finish everything."

"Well then, it sounds as if my timing is good."

"You're timing?"

"I'm off this weekend. I was hoping I could pop down to London to see you."

The thought of seeing Simon was tempting. More than tempting, but I did have a huge paper to write and I knew if he came to London there wasn't much chance that I would be spending my time writing. I sighed. "I would love to see you, but I have to study. I have exams and that paper. It's probably not a good idea."

"I could help you with your studies," he offered.

I dodged around an older couple, trundling slowly along the sidewalk. "Study?" I asked with a snort of disbelief. "You're offering to help me study?"

"If you must know, I was a very serious student while I was at university."

"I'm sure you were, but I don't think that Comparative Religion was part of the program at the RVC."

"Well, I might not know much about the topic, but I could edit your paper for you. Help you polish things up a bit."

I turned the corner onto Rosehill Street and the crowd became noticeably thinner. I started thinking about scones and tea and lovely walks with Simon and I could feel myself weakening. I shook my head. No, I had to write this paper and study. "Simon, I'd love to see you, but I can't." I sighed heavily. "I really have to write this paper. Anyway," I added, "I'll be back at Brynmoor in one week."

"Right. You'll be at Brynmoor, but I'll be in Shawbury."

"Oh, right." I had forgotten that Simon had his own apartment and wasn't living at Brynmoor Manor any longer. The drizzle started coming down harder. "Hold on a minute," I said, juggling the phone and my bags as I pulled the hood of my coat over my head. "Shawbury's not that far. Aren't you coming to Brynmoor for Christmas?" Simon's parents worked for my stepdad, Sir Richard, and lived on his estate. Simon had lived there too, until recently.

"Of course, I am. It's just that I was hoping to enjoy a bit of private time with you before the holidays. Not that I don't love meeting up with you in the stable, but …"

I had a sudden vivid image of Simon just as I had last seen him in September, the afternoon light turning his red hair to gold, the muscles in his arms and back flexing as he tossed fifty-pound sacks of feed from the back of the truck. We had said good-bye the night before, but I was greedy and wanted more time with him. He had jumped down from the back of the truck with a wide grin on his face, scooped me up into his arms, and gave me a good-bye kiss that made my toes curl.

I sighed at the memory, thinking about how very nice it would be to see him this weekend. He was right, with all the holiday preparations and visitors, it was going to be difficult for us to find any private time when I returned to Brynmoor Manor. Maybe a weekend visit from Simon was just the incentive I needed to help me stop procrastinating and finish my paper.

"Hmm," I told him. "I tell you what. Let me see how much work I can get done. I'll go home and start working right now. I'll call you tonight and let you know."

"Right." I could hear the happiness in his voice. "If you put in the work, I'll make it worth your while. I promise."

I laughed. "I know that. It's just I've got so much work to do."

"I told you, I can help edit. I do speak and read the English language quite well."

"I'll keep that in mind."

"If you call me a bit earlier, I can leave right after work." He paused. "I'm willing to sacrifice driving in traffic so I can help edit that paper for you."

"Edit? Hah! I know you, Simon Fitzgibbon. What you really mean is snog."

"Well, if you insist, I might be talked into a bit of snogging."

"You're impossible," I told him, laughing.

"No. I'm in love."

At his words, a warm, happy glow, smooth as warm honey, slid down my spine and settled in my belly. *Okay*, I vowed silently, *no more procrastinating.*

"I'll start working on my paper as soon as I get home," I promised him. "I probably won't get it finished, but if I get a good start on it you can come. I'll call as early as I can, but I warn you, I am probably going to have to work this weekend."

"That's all right. I'll ring one of my mates. Paul would put me up. I can stay at Paul's until you're ready for a study break. I'm awfully good at study breaks, too," he added solemnly.

I laughed. "I bet you are."

"I'll wait for you to ring, then." He paused, before adding, "I miss you."

"I miss you, too," I said, my voice catching a little. At that moment, the clouds opened up and it started to pour. "Simon, I've got to hang up. I'm getting drenched."

"All right then. See you this weekend. Ring me as early as you can."

"I will."

It was really pouring now. I quickly stuffed my phone inside my bag and opened my umbrella. The thought of Simon coming to visit made my heart sing. It was raining in London, but I was walking on sunshine.

Head down, I hurried through the rain. When I turned onto my street, I noticed a man in a long black raincoat standing in front of my apartment building. He had his back to me, but from the way he was waving his arms around, he appeared to be arguing with our doorman, Osmin. Osmin did not look happy. An unhappy Osmin was usually enough to intimidate most people, but I noticed that this man wasn't backing down.

I slowed my steps, torn between my desire to escape the rain and not wanting to get caught in the middle of whatever was going on between Osmin and the man in the black raincoat. The man raised his voice angrily. I couldn't quite catch what he said, but there was no mistaking Osmin's reply. He stood, his body blocking the door, his face impassive, arms across his chest, and shook his head.

I exhaled impatiently. It didn't look like either of the two men was going to back down anytime soon. My shopping bags were getting wet and I had a paper to write.

So, I pasted a pleasant smile on my face and marched up to the front door.

Osmin caught sight of me. "Ah. Here she is now. Miss Lily. You have a visitor."

The man in the black raincoat turned around. I almost dropped my shopping bags in surprise when I saw who it was.

CHAPTER 5

YOU DON'T GET TO CHOOSE YOUR FAMILY

December 6
1:15 p.m.

"Dad?"

My Dad's face creased into a wide smile. "Lily." He strode toward me with open arms, managing to give me an awkward embrace despite my bulky shopping bags and umbrella.

"How is my beautiful girl?"

"What are you doing here?"

"I came to see you."

"Why?"

A hurt expression crossed his face. "What do you mean, why? A father doesn't need a reason to want to see his daughter."

"You flew all the way from California to London just to see me?" I asked in disbelief.

"Well, not just to see you. I am here on business, but that is what made this business deal such a great opportunity. The chance to see you was the bonus that sealed the deal for me."

"What business?" I asked suspiciously.

He gave me a wide smile. The one that made little old ladies twitter and younger women sigh. "I'm involved in a small import/export venture."

"Import/export? Isn't that what all the drug dealers say?" I asked, only half-joking.

He laughed easily. "No drugs, just vodka."

Vodka sounded pretty legit. "What's the name of the company?"

"It's a Russian company, Orlav Vodka Products. You probably haven't heard of them. They market their products under different labels."

"You're right. I've never heard of them. Did you call Mom and tell her you were here?" I asked him, changing the subject. It was always better not to pry too much into my father's business dealings.

"No." He shook his head. "You know how it is between your mother and me."

I did know. My mom had remarried eighteen months ago to an Englishman, a very wealthy Englishman. An English Earl, actually. My father wasn't invited to the wedding.

"So, are you going to ask me in? Or are you going to keep me standing out here in the rain?"

"Uhm, sure." I nodded to Osmin as he held the door open for me. "Thanks, Osmin."

"My pleasure, Miss Lily."

My father acknowledged Osmin with a brusque nod.

"Nice place you've got here," he said, looking around the foyer. "You're pretty lucky. Not every college freshman gets to live in an apartment building with a doorman."

"It's temporary," I told him. I still felt a little defensive about my newly acquired life of privilege. "I applied late for college and university housing was full. Sir Richard is letting me stay in his flat until a spot opens up for me."

"Ah. Sir Richard. Is that what you call him?"

I shrugged.

My dad grinned. "Well, I approve of *Sir Richard's* choice in apartment buildings. Very secure. I tried to get your doorman to let me in so I could wait for you, but he wasn't having any of it. He was very insistent that I remain outside." His eyes flicked in Osmin's direction. Osmin stood erect at his station by the front door, his expression carefully neutral.

"It's Osmin's job to be careful about who gets into the building," I explained.

"Hmm. Well, that's not a bad thing, considering you're living here by yourself. You are living here by yourself, aren't you? No roommates or live-in boyfriends?"

"Are you checking up on me?"

"It's a dad's prerogative."

I rolled my eyes. "No one else lives here. It's just me."

"Good. I can't imagine either your mother or Sir Richard would be very happy if you had a live-in boyfriend hanging around."

"Dad!"

"So, are you going to invite your old man up to your apartment for a cup of that famous English tea? You know. Give your dad a taste of the royal treatment, now that you're hobnobbing with the aristocracy."

"Of course, you can come up," I said as I pushed the button for the elevator. Even though I had just vowed to start working on my paper not less than five minutes earlier, as most people will tell you, it's hard to say no to my dad. It's what makes him a great salesman.

My dad looked around admiring the Art Deco foyer as we waited for the elevator.

The original building had been built in the 1920s. It had survived the bombings of World War II with very little damage. The polished marble floor and crystal chandelier were part of the original building, as were the heavy brass doors. At the moment, the foyer was tastefully decorated for the holidays with a holly wreath and an elegant Christmas tree display with beautifully wrapped presents underneath.

"I see they know how to deck the halls around here," my dad commented. "This is very nice. I am looking forward to seeing your apartment. After all, it's not every day you get to visit a grand duke's apartment."

"He's an earl, Dad, not a duke."

He grinned. "Earl. Duke. It's difficult to keep them all straight, isn't it, when you're just another lowly American?"

"Dad!"

We rode the elevator up to the fourth floor and I let us into the apartment.

"You can hang your coat here," I told him as I folded my umbrella in the brolly stand and shrugged out of my coat, hanging it up on the coat rack. My dad did the same.

My father followed me into the living room and looked around, his gaze taking in the gold-framed oil paintings and antiques. He let out a low appreciative whistle. "This is a nice place. Living in a college dormitory isn't going to be better than this, Tiger Lily. If I were you, I wouldn't be in such a hurry to move out."

I left my soggy shopping bags and my purse on the floor by the couch. "I know it won't be as upscale, but I want to live closer to the campus. Come into the kitchen with me and I'll make us some coffee," I offered.

While I busied myself with the coffee and French press, he sat at the table smiling, his eyes sizing up the appliances, the copper pots hanging from the rack over the stove, and the Wedgewood china.

The truth was, I wasn't sure how I felt about my father

showing up. He'd had plenty of opportunities to visit me when my mom and I had been living in LA, but he rarely did. And now here he was, sitting in my kitchen and acting as if he visited me every week when, in fact, I hadn't seen the man since … I had to stop and think. Since my sixteenth birthday, nearly two and half years ago. And that last visit hadn't gone well.

Just like today, my father had unexpectedly shown up at our apartment, the one I shared with my mother and grandmother. My mom and grandmother had planned to take me out for my birthday dinner to my favorite restaurant. I had been so thrilled to see my dad that I barely registered the unhappy glances my mother and grandmother exchanged before reluctantly inviting him to join us.

"Order anything you want on the menu, ladies," he'd told me. "After all, a sweet sixteen only comes once in a lifetime." He encouraged me to order abalone appetizers and lobster for dinner because I had never tried them before. He ordered champagne for the adults.

I have to admit, my dad had been the life of the party. He told amusing stories and made me laugh so hard that I snorted my iced tea, which made us laugh even harder. He encouraged the waiters and the entire restaurant to sing happy birthday to me. It was wonderful; I felt like a royal princess. It was probably one of the best birthdays I ever had, until the bill arrived.

My father had conveniently forgotten his wallet, leaving my mother and grandmother to pay for our extravagantly expensive dinner. I still remember the look of worry on my mother's face as she pulled out her credit card. I knew that we couldn't afford lobster and champagne, and I felt terribly guilty for ordering such an expensive meal. I wouldn't have ordered those things if my father hadn't encouraged me. I think that was the day I finally realized that I was more grown up than my dad. And now here he was, waltzing into my life as if he had never left.

My dad settled into his chair at the kitchen table. "So, how have you been?" he asked, as I filled the kettle with water and turned on the stove.

"You mean since the last time I saw you?" I asked, unable to mask the resentment I was feeling. Of course, the minute the words were out of my mouth, I felt bad about it. After all, my dad was making an effort to come visit me.

My dad picked up on the resentment in my tone of voice. "Hey, Tiger Lily, it sounds like I've caught you at a bad time. Maybe I should take a raincheck on that coffee." He started to rise from his chair.

I let out an exasperated sigh. "No. Don't go," I said quickly, feeling guilty. "I'm sorry. Stay and have some coffee," I offered with an apologetic smile. "I wasn't expecting to see you and …" I paused, unsure how I wanted to finish that sentence.

My dad settled back in his seat.

I turned my back on him and spooned the coffee grounds into the French press without saying anything. I didn't want to send him away, but I wasn't ready to forgive him either. I don't think he had any idea how hurtful it was to have a dad who considered you an afterthought. I mean, the man pretty much dropped out of my life after my parents divorced. My mom used to say that my dad always had a good story and an even better excuse.

"Lily, I know I've been a lousy father these past few years, but I'd like to make it up to you. Maybe we can spend some time together while I'm in England, if you're willing?"

I fitted the lid on top before slowly turning around to face him.

My dad looked at me hopefully. "What do you say?"

I sighed. My father wasn't really a bad man. He just happened to be a lousy father. Mostly because he was too self-centered and too irresponsible to be a good one. That was just who he was. He was never going to change, but I knew that, in his own way, he did love me.

"Well, I would like to, but right now I'm pretty busy."

"I understand." He nodded slowly. "Well, we'll just have to make the most of this visit then. Won't we?"

I felt another twinge of guilt. I placed two mugs on the table and sat down. "I'm getting ready for finals, Dad. But I'm sure we can work something out while you're here." My dad grinned and reached over, placing his hand on top of mine.

"That's my girl," he said. "So, now that you've forgiven your old man, how about opening your Christmas present?" He took a small box out of his pocket and handed it to me.

"You brought me a Christmas present?" I asked.

"Of course I did." He grinned like a young boy. "Go ahead. Open it. No need to wait for Christmas."

"Are you sure?"

"Absolutely."

I untied the ribbon and opened the box. Inside was a silver bracelet. A series of tiny swallows in flight linked by a delicate chain rested on the blue velvet lining.

"It's beautiful."

"I knew you would like it. I bought it in an antique store. I thought it looked like you."

"Thanks, Dad. It's really beautiful." I took it out of the box and held it up, admiring the way that the light reflected on the silver birds. It made them look as if they were flying.

"I knew it would be perfect for you," he said, looking pleased. "Merry Christmas, Tiger Lily."

I couldn't help but smile as I fastened the bracelet around my wrist. "It's not exactly Christmas yet," I teased.

"Well then, Merry early Christmas."

CHAPTER 6

KNOCK, KNOCK. WHO'S THERE?

December 7
8:00 a.m.

Simon woke feeling energized and upbeat. He tossed a few things in his bag and, whistling cheerfully, drove to the corner bakery, smiling at the thought of having breakfast with Lily. The scones were a peace offering since he was probably going to arrive before she woke. A self-serving peace offering, since he also knew she wouldn't have much more than coffee and yogurt in her kitchen.

He hummed along with the radio as he eased onto the A53, happy she'd agreed to have him visit. It was a bit mad to drive all that distance for a couple of days, especially when she would be in Brynmoor in less than a week, but he really did want to have some private time with her. Once she was back at the manor house, there wouldn't be much opportunity for privacy. Between the holiday, her family, his family, and his work, they would be lucky if they managed a night to themselves. Yes, the long drive was definitely worth it.

When he arrived at her building, he keyed in the security code and pulled into the parking garage, slipping his car into Lord Yarlbury's parking space with a momentary pang of conscience. He didn't think Lord Yarlbury would be visiting London this weekend, but just to be on the safe side, he made a mental note to check with Lily.

He rode the lift up to the fourth floor, smiling in anticipation. She had left the front door open and unlocked for him. *So much for waking her up*, he thought as he pushed the door open.

"Lily. I've brought you breakfast," he called out.

He paused just inside the door and waited. When she didn't answer, he called out again, "Lily?"

No answer. Perhaps she wasn't awake after all. He grinned. He was more than up to the task of awakening a Sleeping Beauty. He dropped his bag on the floor. After placing the box of scones on the sofa table, he tiptoed into her bedroom.

The bedroom was empty. Her bed had been slept in, but she was gone. He knocked on the bathroom door, checked the kitchen, and searched the other rooms. Puzzled, he wondered where she had gone. Perhaps she'd left to run some errands. His mouth twitched. She'd probably gone out to buy scones. The two of them must have been thinking the same thing. He sent a message to her mobile. No answer.

No bother. He was happy to wait. More than likely, she'd be home before the kettle whistled. He tossed his overnight bag into her room and carried the box of scones into the kitchen. A French press and two coffee cups sat invitingly on the table. He smiled.

He started to pour himself a cup of coffee before realizing that both of the mugs were dirty. He touched the French press. It was cold.

Apparently, he wasn't her first visitor this morning. Whoever it was must have shown up quite early. Deciding that even if she'd already had her morning coffee, he could use a cup of something hot to drink, he washed out the French press and the two mugs and placed them on the drainboard. He filled the kettle with water and placed it on the stove. He would have everything prepared before she returned.

CHAPTER 7

THE PLAN

1943
Summer

Realistically, Heinrich knew that the odds of making it to England were not in his favor. Two months ago, the body of a man had washed up along the south end of the island, drowned while trying to escape from a neighboring island. Heinrich had seen his bloated body.

Sixty miles of strong currents, rough seas, and treacherous open water lay between Alderney Island and England. If the German patrols caught him, he would be convicted as a traitor and shot by a firing squad. If the English caught him, there was a high probability that they would shoot him, also. It was a dangerous plan, but Heinrich was willing to take the risk.

He began his preparations just before Christmas, spending months rowing around the island in one of the many small boats the German patrols had confiscated from the locals. Every free afternoon, Heinrich rowed along the coast searching for a place to stash a boat and supplies for his escape. The other guards had laughed at him, addressing him mockingly as *Meermeister.* He found it easy to smile back at them because he knew he would have the last laugh when he reached England. He'd grin and give them a jaunty wave each time he rowed away from the dock.

It took him months, but he finally found it, a small rocky cove with a shallow cave located just above the high tide mark. The cave, impossible to see from the road, had just enough room inside to stash a small boat.

By the beginning of June, he was ready to put his plan into action. Borrowing an eight-foot boat with a small outboard motor, Heinrich rowed away from the dock, waving merrily to the guards. When he reached the cove, he lugged the boat onto the shore and secured it in the small cave camouflaging it with brush and driftwood. Next, he dove into the frigid water, making sure that he was completely soaked.

Shivering, he clambered up the cliff to the road, slipping and sliding as loose dirt and rocks tumbled down into the ocean below. He carefully marked the spot by building a small cairn of rocks before beginning the long walk back to the camp.

Hours later, he arrived at the camp, exhausted and sunburned. No one doubted his story about the boat springing a leak and sinking. He endured the heckling of the other guards with a smile. Everyone thought it was very funny that the *Meermeister* had sunk his boat.

During the next few weeks, he continued to return the cove ferrying stolen supplies to his boat by bicycle. By July, he was ready. He shouldered the last of his supplies in his bulging rucksack and hopped on a bicycle. By now, the tale of his sinking ship had made the rounds.

"You're off on another one of your excursions, are

you? I see you've given up your sea mania for a bicycle. We will have to change your name to *Fahrradmeister* soon," the gate guard remarked as he raised the barrier for Heinrich.

Heinrich shrugged. "I like the exercise," he commented companionably.

"At least this time, if you spring a leak you won't get wet," the guard said with a laugh.

Heinrich smiled good-naturedly as he pedaled past.

When he reached the cairn marking the location of the cove, he hopped off the bike and hid it in the brush before carefully scrambling down the rock face. He changed from his Nazi uniform into the English clothes he had stolen from an abandoned house, shivering as the sweat on his skin cooled quickly in the late afternoon air. He buried his uniform under the sand at the back of the cave and dumped his rucksack into the bottom of the boat. Then he sat and waited for the sun to set.

When the last of the light faded from the sky, Heinrich ventured outside his cave. The night sky enveloped in a velvety darkness illuminated only by the faint light of stars and a wafer-thin, crescent moon. It was time.

He dragged the boat out of the cave onto the rocky beach, pushing it into the ocean. He didn't let himself think about what he was doing. If he did, he wasn't sure he would have the courage to continue. The frigid ocean water quickly turned his legs and feet numb as he waded through the waves. When he was clear of the rocks, he jumped in, fit the oars in the oarlocks, and began rowing toward England. The simple rhythm of rowing helped to quiet his fear.

Despite his desire to get as far away as quickly as possible, he didn't use the boat's outboard motor. He didn't want to take the chance of a curious sea patrol hearing the sound of his motor and coming to investigate.

The air grew colder as the hours passed and his hands grew numb, but he kept a steady rhythm: catch, pull, recover. The hypnotic movement carried him past tiredness. He lost consciousness of the passing of time. Catch, pull, recover. Catch, pull, recover. Catch, pull, recover. He focused his attention on the sigh of breath as it moved in and out of his lungs, the contraction of his muscles, the creak of the oars, the soft rhythmic splashing of water against wood as he rowed farther and farther from Alderney Island.

Eventually, as if waking from a half-sleep, he noticed the sea growing choppier. Icy water spilled over the gunwales and sprayed him. He rested the oars in the oarlocks and sat quietly drifting for several minutes. He listened, straining his ears for the sound of a patrol boat's motor. He heard nothing but the sound of the waves slapping against the hull. He saw nothing but the dark sea. It was time to use the outboard motor.

On his first attempt, the motor didn't catch. He felt a moment's panic knife through him. Without the motor, he would not be able to get far enough from the island to avoid the German patrol boats. He yanked hard on the starter cord a second time. The motor spluttered to life. Inhaling with relief, he settled himself on the hard plank seat, keeping one hand on the tiller, and checked his compass. He was on his way to England!

CHAPTER 8

THE INSPECTOR

December 7
12:30 p.m.

Simon finished his cup of tea and poured himself another. He carried it into the living room with a second scone. He couldn't imagine what was taking Lily so long.

When the doorbell rang, he assumed that Lily had forgotten her key. He stood, calling out something about not leaving doors unlocked because you never knew who might show up, before opening the door with an expectant grin on his face.

Instead of Lily standing in the hall, he found himself staring at a very serious uniformed police constable and a man in a suit and tie.

"Good morning. I'm Detective Chief Inspector Shah," the man in the suit said, introducing himself to Simon with a reassuring smile. He held up his warrant card. "This is Constable Williams. We'd like to have a word with Lily

Deene, if possible."

"You want to speak with Lily?" Simon asked, puzzled.

"Yes."

"She's not in at the moment."

"I see. Do you happen to know where she is?" the police inspector asked pleasantly.

Simon shook his head. "No. Why are you looking for Lily?"

Again, the police inspector's white teeth flashed amiably. "Why don't we come in so that we can sort things properly?" He stepped toward the door as if to enter the flat.

Simon did not move. "Why don't you tell me what this is about," he countered, blocking the entrance. "And then I'll call Lord Yarlbury and ask him if he's comfortable with you coming into his flat to sort things properly."

Inspector Shah's eyes locked onto Simon. He was no longer smiling. "Funny you should mention Lord Yarlbury, as he called this morning and asked that I check on his stepdaughter. I was led to believe that she lived here alone. So, why don't we start with your name, and then you can tell me what it is you are doing in his lordship's flat?"

"Simon Fitzgibbon."

Inspector Shah nodded politely as Simon stood to one side to allow the inspector to enter the flat.

"I don't understand. Why did Lord Yarlbury ask the police to check on Lily?" Simon asked.

"His lordship requested a welfare check on his stepdaughter. Her family is concerned."

Something cold sliced through Simon. "A welfare check? Why? Is she all right?"

Inspector Shah gazed at Simon for a moment. "That is what we are trying to determine. We are hoping to locate your friend. Do you have any idea where she might be?

Simon shook his head. "No, I don't. I was supposed to meet her here, but she wasn't home. Has something happened to Lily?"

"As I said, that is what we are trying to determine at the moment. Now, if you would sit down, Mr. Fitzgibbon, and answer my questions, we can get on with things."

Simon remained standing as he held the inspector's gaze. None of this made any sense.

"If you are concerned about your friend, then the best thing you can do to help her is to cooperate with us."

Simon sat on the sofa.

"Thank you. Is there anyone who might know if Lily has gone off somewhere for the weekend?"

"She wouldn't have gone anywhere. We had plans."

"Perhaps she had a change of plans."

"No. She messaged me last night. She knew I was coming."

The police inspector fixed his gaze on Simon for a moment as if gauging the truthfulness of his statement.

"Very good. You received a message from her last night. That was the last time you heard from her?"

Simon nodded. "Yes. She sent me a message. That's why I drove down to see her this morning."

"May I see your mobile, please?" Inspector Shah held out his hand expectantly.

Simon silently handed his mobile.

"Thank you." Shah took it, glanced down, and quickly scrolled through the messages and phone log while Simon watched. When he finished, he looked up. "What time did you arrive?" he asked.

Simon stared at him for a moment before answering. "Half eleven or thereabout."

"She knew you were planning to visit?"

"Yes. I've already told you. We talked about it. You've seen the message. Why does Lord Yarlbury think she's gone missing?"

The inspector ignored Simon's question. "Lily wasn't here when you arrived at the flat?"

"No. Again, I've already told you."

"How did you get into the flat, then? Do you have a

key?"

"The door was open."

"Open?"

"Just a bit." Simon held up his hands, leaving a space of about three inches between them.

"Does she normally leave the door open like that?"

He gave his head another little shake. "No. I thought she'd left it open for me. That she'd stepped out for something. Maybe to buy a pint of milk or some scones. I thought she'd left it open because she didn't want me to have to wait in the hall."

"How did the flat look when you arrived?"

"It looked like this," Simon answered with a sweep of his arm.

"No signs of a struggle, overturned furniture, anything like that?"

"No."

"All right, then," Inspector Shah said with a quick nod of his head. "Do you know of anyone who might have his lordship's number and could have called him about his daughter?"

"What? What do you mean, call him about his daughter? Has someone called Lord Yarlbury? What did they say about Lily?"

"If you would answer the question, please."

Simon's chest suddenly felt unbearably tight, as if there was an iron band around it. He tried to breathe, but his lungs didn't seem to be able to take in any air. He forced himself to inhale deeply, exhaling slowly. "Please. Tell me what's happened to Lily."

Inspector Shah sighed. "At the moment, we don't know that anything *has* happened to her. However, Lord Yarlbury received a phone call this morning demanding a ransom payment for the safe return of his stepdaughter. When he was unable to ring her on her mobile or at the flat, he called and asked us to check on her."

"But that's mad! It doesn't make any sense," Simon

said. “A ransom demand? You think Lily’s been kidnapped?”

“Well, we don’t know for certain that she’s been abducted. It might be a hoax.” Inspector Shah gazed at Simon with narrowed, thoughtful eyes. “I noticed you have Lord Yarlbury’s number in your contacts.”

“What?” Simon asked, confused by the sudden change in topic.

“Why do you have his lordship’s number in your contacts?”

“I work for him. Worked for him,” he corrected. “His groom was injured. I helped with horses until the groom was able to come back to work. Why does it matter that I have his phone number?”

Inspector Shah shrugged. “It’s an unlisted number, yet the person who demanded the ransom was able to call him on it.”

Simon raked his fingers through his hair and stared in disbelief at the police inspector. “You think I called Lord Yarlbury? And what? Told him that I kidnapped Lily? That’s daft!”

“There were no outgoing calls to his number from your mobile, but you could have had someone else make the call.”

Anger and resentment at the ridiculous accusation boiled up inside of Simon. He inhaled deeply again and held the air in his lungs for a moment before speaking slowly and clearly. “I did *not* ring Lord Yarlbury. Nor did I ask someone to ring Lord Yarlbury.”

“All right then. Is there anyone else she might be visiting? Someone she may have called perhaps and mentioned her change of plans?”

“I don’t know.” Simon raked his hands through his hair again. “She just started at the university this term. I don’t know many of her friends in London.” He paused, thinking. “She might have called Jenna.”

“Jenna?”

"My sister. They're best mates."

"Why don't you call your sister, then? Ask if she has heard from Lily recently." Inspector Shah paused. "It would be best if you don't mention that we are looking for her. We don't want to alarm anyone unnecessarily."

Simon nodded, then punched Jenna's number. The police inspector listened intently as he spoke to Jenna.

"Simon?" Jenna's voice sounded surprised when she answered the phone.

"Hullo, Jenna."

"Why are you ringing me? Is everything all right?"

"Yeah. Everything's fine. I was just wondering if you chatted with Lily this week."

"No. Why?"

"I popped in to see her and she's not in."

"She's probably studying. It is the last week of term, you know. Some of us have exams."

"Right." Simon forced himself to smile. "I best leave you to it then." He hung up, giving his head a quick shake. "She hasn't heard from her either."

Inspector Shah handed a card to Simon. "This is my office number and my mobile. If you hear from Lily, or if you think of any other information that might be of use, please contact me immediately."

Simon nodded numbly before closing the door behind the two men.

He sat on the sofa, dazed, staring at nothing. It had been more than three hours since he arrived in London, and Lily had yet to appear at the front door of the flat. With each passing minute, his hope that she was going to walk through that door faded. A feeling of dread settled in the pit of his stomach, twisting his intestines and pushing them up against the bottom of his lungs.

The worst of it was that there was nothing he could do but wait. Bloody hell! Desperate to do something, he pulled his mobile from his pocket and punched in her number. He waited, listening as it went to voice message.

"Hey, I can't answer the phone right now. Leave a message at the beep."

The sound of her voice caused a jolt of pain at the base of his throat. "Lily," he said, his voice catching. He found that he didn't know what to say. "I love you," he whispered.

CHAPTER 9

ROW, ROW, ROW YOUR BOAT

1943
Summer

Heinrich pushed the little craft through the choppy seas for several hours before stopping the engine to refill it with petrol. The sky was beginning to turn a thin watery gray at the edges. It was almost morning. He was physically tired, yet also strangely energized.

Taking a quick break to drink thirstily from his water jug, he wolfed down half a loaf of stale bread and a hunk of hard cheese. His little boat rose and fell on the surging waves as he poured the petrol into the engine. Water sloshed over the bow collecting in the bottom of the boat. Belatedly, he realized that he should have brought something with him to bail water. He eyed the puddle of seawater for a moment. There was nothing he could do about it now, except hope that he reached England before it became a problem. He yanked the starter cord and once again aimed the bow toward the English shore.

As the small boat pushed its way through the waves, the wind increased in strength. Heinrich nervously eyed the dark clouds gathering overhead. It looked like there might be some rain coming his way. He kept a firm hand on the tiller as the sea pitched and rolled with increasing violence beneath his little boat.

By late morning, he knew he was in trouble. The sky had grown so dark that it was almost impossible to see where the sky ended and the slate-colored sea began. He swore and tightened his grip on the tiller, checked his compass once again, and resolutely kept his little boat pointed toward England.

The storm broke with a howl and a roar. Lightning forked and slashed across the sky like white cannon fire as thunder boomed and cracked around him. Wind-driven rain needled his exposed skin like sharp shards of glass. He fought to hold the tiller steady as the storm raged around him, turning the sea into the churning frothing mass of icy dark water, tossing his small boat among the surging waves like a child's toy. A violent wave hit him broadside and the small boat pitched and rolled, coming dangerously close to capsizing as ice-cold water sloshed over the gunwales drenching him and the outboard motor. The engine died.

Shivering with cold, Heinrich hunched over the outboard motor and yanked on the starter cord as the boat spun and rolled in the roiling sea. Nothing happened.

He pulled the cord a second time, then a third and fourth time. The engine wouldn't start. Knowing that he needed to turn the boat into the waves or risk capsizing, he grabbed the oars. Somehow, he managed to fit them into the oarlocks as the boat spun and pitched and rolled beneath him. Fighting the wind, the boat riding dangerously low in the water, he began to row.

Catch. Pull. Recover. Catch. Pull. Recover. He gave up all hope of navigating. He put all of his effort into keeping his small craft afloat. Half-frozen, his eyes burning from the salt spray, his hands bloody and raw, Heinrich rowed. He rowed because he had no choice. He rowed because if he stopped rowing he would die.

CHAPTER 10

THE LORD AND LADY ARRIVE

December 7
5:00 p.m.

Simon had held onto the hope that it was all a mistake. He sat, rigid and unmoving, his fists clenched, his neck and shoulders tense as he stared at his phone willing it to ring. Willing Lily to call and laughingly tell him that it had all been a mistake. Willing her to walk through the door of the flat. He couldn't bring himself to leave because that meant admitting that she wasn't coming back to the flat.

As the minutes ticked by, he moved from denial to fear, from fear to anger. Someone had done this terrible thing to Lily! Some unknown person had taken her. Was she hurt? God! Please don't let him hurt her! Anger, hot and bitter, rose in the back of his throat. He wanted to hunt down the person who had done this to her and rip him limb from limb, and yet he could do nothing but sit and wait. The knowledge that he was powerless to help her tore him to pieces! He closed his eyes, shaking with effort to keep his emotions under control.

Simon became aware of noise in the hallway outside of the flat, footsteps, voices speaking softly. The police? Had they returned? Had they found Lily? He turned to face the door and listened. He heard the metallic clink of keys and stood abruptly, his heart lifting, bumping painfully against his ribs.

"Lily?" he called out.

The door opened.

Lord Yarlbury stood in the hallway, eyebrows rising slightly in surprise upon seeing him. "Simon? You gave me a bit of a start."

"Sorry, Sir. I should have left after the police, but …" He trailed off.

Lord Yarlbury held up a hand to stop Simon from apologizing. "No. I'm glad that you're here. We're glad you're here," he amended, holding the door open for Lily's mother. She entered carrying Lily's baby brother, Will.

Lily's mother looked as if she might shatter at the slightest touch. When she saw Simon, her mouth trembled.

"Simon, did the police say anything? Do they know who did this? Do they know where she is?" she asked, her voice shaking a little, needing something, anything that would help her believe that Lily was safe.

She looked at him with such hope and fear that it made Simon's heart lurch. His throat constricted. Not trusting himself to speak, he gave his head a little shake.

Her expression crumpled and she bowed over Will's small, fuzzy head concealing the shimmer of tears in her eyes.

Lord Yarlbury gazed at his wife with a mixture of love and concern. There were worry lines etched into his face that Simon had never noticed before. "The London police are very good at what they do," Lord Yarlbury told her confidently. "I intend to make certain they put their best man on this. We'll get her back." He laid a gentle, comforting hand on her back.

Simon found himself wanting to believe him also.

"Why don't you get Will settled, my dear? Simon and I can fetch the rest of the luggage." Lord Yarlbury glanced inquiringly at Simon. "If you don't mind lending a hand that is."

"I'd be happy to help, Sir," Simon replied, grateful for the distraction. Doing something, anything, was better than thinking about Lily and witnessing Lady Yarlbury's distress.

Lady Yarlbury gave Simon a ghost of a smile. "Thank you, Simon. What would we do without the Fitzgibbon family?" she added, her voice soft as a whisper, before drifting into the bedroom with Will.

Simon followed Lily's stepfather out of the apartment to the elevators.

They stood shoulder to shoulder, staring at the closed doors of the lift in a tense, awkward silence.

"Sorry about the car, Sir," Simon said after a moment.

"The car?" Lord Yarlbury asked distractedly.

"I've parked my car in your spot in the garage. I'll move it as soon as I've helped with the luggage."

His lordship waved a dismissive hand. "There's no need to worry. I've asked Osmin to wait with the car so that I could escort Lady Yarlbury to the flat. This business …" He paused and closed his eyes. He cleared his throat and started again. "As you can imagine, Lady Yarlbury is very distressed, and I thought it would be best to take her up to the flat straight away," he said briskly. "The important thing right now is to do everything we can to ensure that Lily is returned quickly. The police tell me that the fact that they are asking for a ransom is a good thing. That it means she is still …" He broke off suddenly. He didn't finish the sentence. He didn't need to.

Not trusting his voice, Simon nodded that he understood.

The elevator arrived and the doors opened. Lord

Yarlbury turned toward Simon. "Simon, I don't know what your plans are, but I would greatly appreciate it if you would be willing to stay at the flat for a while longer. As you can see, her ladyship is in a fragile state. I have to go out. I've details that must be sorted rather quickly, and I am uncomfortable leaving her alone. I would be very grateful if you could stay with her until I return."

"Of course. I'm happy to stay as long as you need me to."

"Thank you." Lord Yarlbury managed a grim smile. "As her ladyship so aptly noted, what would we do without the Fitzgibbon family?"

Simon made tea in the kitchen while Lady Yarlbury set up the portable crib in the bedroom for Will. He could hear her talking and singing softly to him, soothing herself as well as the baby. He filled the kettle and put it on the stove to boil. Opening cabinets, he searched for the tea set. Once he found it, he filled the sugar bowl and poured some milk into the pitcher. It was strangely comforting, this routine act of making tea.

All at once, he was struck by the sudden memory of making tea and Lily laughing and telling him how the first thing the English do in any emergency was to put the kettle on. Overcome, he sat at the kitchen table and rested his head in his hands.

By the time the tea was ready, he felt steadier, able to cope with Lady Yarlbury's distress as well as his own. Will was settled in his crib and Lady Yarlbury sat alone on the sofa. She gave Simon a wobbly smile when he offered her a cup of tea and a scone. "Thank you."

"I heard you singing to Will," he said. "I didn't recognize the song."

"It's lullaby *Mon Petit.* I used to sing that same song to Lily when she was a baby." She closed her eyes for a moment as if she was in pain. "I think it's Canadian, but

I'm not sure."

Simon nodded and sat in the armchair across from her. They sipped their tea in silence while the scones sat untouched on the plates.

"They called Richard from Lily's phone," Lady Yarlbury said suddenly. "Richard answered it because he thought it was Lily calling. It wasn't. It was a man's voice. He said he had Lily, and if we wanted to see her again, we would have to pay."

The hand holding her teacup shook. She carefully set it down on the saucer.

"That was all. He hung up. Richard tried to call Lily's phone, but it was disconnected."

Tears filled her eyes and began to roll silently down her cheeks. She did nothing to stop them. "Oh, Simon, they have my daughter and there is nothing I can do but wait and hope that they will give her back to me."

He stared at Lily's mother. Fear and anger churned inside of him, forming a tight hard ball in the pit of his stomach. "We'll get her back," he said resolutely. "Whatever it takes. We will find her and bring her back."

"I don't know what to do. I think if I …"

The shrill ring of the phone made them both jump. They sat and stared dumbly at it as it rang a second time.

"Would you like me to answer for you?"

Lady Yarlbury took a moment to collect herself. She brushed away her tears, then with a sharp intake of breath, picked up the receiver.

"Hello."

She listened to the person speaking on the other end. It didn't take long. "Thank you, Osmin."

She slowly replaced the handset. "The police are on their way up," she said. "They didn't say what they wanted. Do you think they've discovered something?" she asked anxiously.

Simon glanced at the door. "I expect we'll find out soon enough."

"Oh, I wish Richard were here." Lady Yarlbury's voice trembled and her hands fluttered about her like two lost birds before settling once again in her lap. Tears welled up in her eyes. "I'm not sure I'm up to meeting with them. What if …" She let her sentence trail off, unable to complete it.

"Why don't you refill the kettle?" Simon suggested. "I'll see what they want and can tell them to come back later after Lord Yarlbury returns."

She nodded gratefully. "Oh, thank you, Simon. I just can't face them right now."

Simon stood. "I'm certain they'll understand."

She went into the kitchen and Simon could hear the sounds of water running as she filled the tea kettle. Like Lady Yarlbury, he wondered why the police were returning so soon. Had they found something new? Had the person who had taken Lily called a second time? Is that why Lord Yarlbury went out? The muscles in his neck and shoulders bunched together, tense with anxiety as he stood by the front door.

The bell rang. Simon let out a long, slow steadying breath before opening the door.

Inspector Shah stood in the hallway with another man. Like Shah, the man was not wearing a uniform. In contrast to the compact Shah, this man was tall, only an inch or so shorter than Simon. There was something vaguely familiar about him, though Simon couldn't quite place him. He didn't look like a police inspector, but then again, he supposed if a police inspector wanted to wear a gold pinky ring and a flashy gold watch, there was no law against it.

Inspector Shah nodded politely to Simon.

"Who are you?" the second man asked rudely, his accent American. He turned toward the inspector. "Who is this guy? One of yours?"

"This is Mr. Fitzgibbon," Inspector Shah replied. He turned to face Simon. "Mr. Fitzgibbon, would you be so kind as to let Lord Yarlbury know that I am here? I should like to have a word with Lordship and Lady Yarlbury."

"Lord Yarlbury's gone out. Lady Yarlbury is here, but she isn't able to meet with you just now."

"What is that supposed to mean?" the man standing next to Shah asked, his expression belligerent. "Maggie?" He called out. "Maggie!" He tried to step through the doorway, but Simon blocked his path.

"What the hell!" He pulled up short, staring at Simon. "Fine! I can stand out here in the hallway and make myself heard if that is what you prefer. "Maggie!" the man shouted. "I know you're here! I want to talk to you!"

Hearing the noise, Lady Yarlbury came out of the kitchen. When she caught sight of the unknown man, she gasped, her hand covering her mouth like an old-fashioned movie actress.

"David? What are you doing here?"

Puzzled, Simon turned back to look at the man standing next to Shah.

"Our daughter's been kidnapped and you don't even have the decency to pick up the phone to tell me!" the man accused her.

It took a moment, but Simon suddenly realized why the man looked vaguely familiar—he was Lily's father. Now that he knew who the man was, he could see the resemblance. He had the same wavy dark hair and long, straight nose as his daughter.

"I … I didn't know you were in England."

David Deene pushed past Simon.

"What difference does that make? You should have called me! Our daughter has been kidnapped!"

"Mr. Deene …" Inspector Shah tried to interject.

David Deene ignored him. He continued berating Lady Yarlbury. "You sent our daughter to London by herself! What were you thinking? She's a young girl! You should never have left California! If you had stayed where you belonged, this never would have happened!"

Lady Yarlbury closed her eyes for a moment as if

collecting herself. "David, please," she said quietly. "I know you're upset. It's understandable. We're all upset."

"Really? I'm glad you think I am entitled to be upset!" he spat out, his eyes darting around the room, daring someone to challenge him. "Since it is *my daughter* that has gone missing. I can't believe I had to find out from the *god damn doorman*! When were you going to call me, Maggie? When?"

Lady Yarlbury looked away.

"You weren't going to call, were you?" David Deene accused her. "Our daughter is missing, and you weren't going to tell me. Funny. I wonder if you would even have known she was missing if the scum who took her hadn't called? You sent our daughter to live in London alone! She's only eighteen! How could you? What kind of mother are you!"

Simon glanced over at Lily's mother. The color had drained from her face and she swayed slightly as if she had been physically struck. He quickly crossed the room, grasped her elbow to steady her before turning to give Lily's father an icy stare.

"Mr. Deene," Inspector Shah said sharply with a glance at Lily's mother. "This is not helping matters. Kindly restrain yourself."

David Deene whipped around and glared at the inspector. "My daughter is missing! Don't tell me to restrain myself!"

Simon could feel Lady Yarlbury trembling beside him. He felt his own temper rising hot and bright.

"Mr. Deene, casting blame is not going to help bring your daughter back. We need to focus on finding her," Inspector Shah said.

"Then why aren't you doing that?" David Deene's voice grew louder. "Why are you here, *instead of looking for my daughter*?"

The shouting woke Will, his wail rose from the bedroom. Lady Yarlbury turned abruptly and fled to the other room.

"That's right! Go ahead and take care of your new son while our daughter is God knows where!" Deene shouted.

Anger surged through Simon like an electrical current, but he forced himself to be calm. After all, this was Lily's father. He said slowly and carefully to David Deene, "You need to leave." He turned toward Shah. "Inspector Shah, I'll let Lord Yarlbury know you were here. I think it would best if you both left now."

"I'm not leaving! No butler is going to tell me what to do! Not when it's *my daughter* who's been kidnapped! I want to know what you people are doing to find her!"

"Mr. Deene." Inspector Shah gave Lily's father a steely stare. "I think it would be best for you to accompany me to the station. I'll need your statement about your visit with your daughter. I think it would be best that we do this now." He stepped back from the doorway and held the door wide. "You may follow me down to the station, or if you prefer, I can have one of the constables escort you."

Breathing heavily, Deene managed to get his temper under control. "Fine," David Deene spat out. "Let's get this done." Eyes narrowed, he threw an angry, resentful look at Simon. "Tell her *ladyship* that I'll be back to talk to her after I finish with the police." He spun on his heel and strode out the door.

Inspector Shah acknowledged Simon with a brief nod before leaving.

Simon closed the door behind them. He had always imagined Lily's father was a proper arse. David Deene had just confirmed it.

CHAPTER 11

THE ICE CHEST

December 7
7:00 p.m.

I opened my eyes once again to complete unyielding darkness. I didn't know if I'd been asleep for fifteen minutes or fifteen hours. My mouth felt as if I had been chewing sand, but the fog in my brain seemed to have dissipated.

Very slowly, very gingerly, I sat up. My stomach heaved. I covered my mouth, trembling with the effort to keep from being physically sick again. Were they looking for me? Simon? My mother? Sir Richard? Had they called the police? How would the police find me? How would anyone know where to find me? The thought that I might not see any of them again left me struggling for breath as if my heart was being crushed under a heavy weight.

"I am here with you." Harry's voice was comforting.

"Harry?" I rasped.

"I am here."

I sat up slowly and wrapped my arms around my knees. My head throbbed. My throat felt as if it had been scraped raw. "I want to go home," I whimpered.

"*Ja.* You miss your family, but you must be strong," Harry said. "You must be strong for your family."

I thought of my mother and my baby brother, Will. I thought of Simon. Sir Richard. Mrs. and Mr. Fitzgibbon. Jenna. I knew that every one of them would be doing everything in their power to help me. I rested my chin on my knees and took a shaky breath.

"I can be strong," I said after a moment.

"*Ja.* That is good."

"How long will he keep me here?"

"I do not know."

"Okay." I breathed deeply trying to calm myself as I reasoned aloud, more for my benefit than Harry's. "Most likely what they want is money. As soon as they get their money, I can go home. All I need to do is stay calm and wait, and as soon as the ransom is paid, I will be able to go home again."

"Yes," Harry said approvingly. "You will be strong. He brings you food and water. He does not want to harm you. He wants money. You will go home when he has money. Now, you must eat and drink to make you strong."

"How …" I started to ask, then I remembered the cooler. The man had shoved an ice chest into the room. There was an ice chest somewhere in here with me. I licked my dry, cracked lips. "Is there water in the ice chest?"

"*Ja.* Yes. Food and drink to make you strong."

I stared blindly in the darkness. Where was it? Turning my head, I tried to remember. He had opened the door and shoved it across the floor. Where was the door? The blackness was so complete that I couldn't see even the faintest outline of the cooler or the door or anything else.

"You will look. You will find it."

"I don't know," I replied uncertainly. "It's so dark. I can't see anything."

"Yes. You can find the food and water."

I hesitated, peering into the nothingness. My stomach squeezed into a tight little ball of anxiety. I still felt dizzy and disoriented. I tried to psyche myself up, knowing I needed to take that first step into the empty vastness that surrounded me.

"You are a brave girl. You can do this," Harry encouraged me.

"Okay. I can do this," I said aloud. I took another shaky breath and pushed the hair out of my eyes. I needed to move. I needed to find the ice chest.

"Okay. Harry, I'm going to try and find the ice chest," I told him as I tried to convince myself to begin.

"That is good."

"Okay. Here I go." With a last deep breath, I pushed onto my knees and crawled forward. The darkness seemed to dip and rise about me like waves in an ocean. My stomach lurched.

"Harry?" I cried out.

"*Ja*. Yes. Keep going."

Slowly, carefully, I crawled. Blindly patting the ground in front of me with my hands as I inched my way through. I moved tentatively over the uneven brick surface. My lack of vision was disorienting. I had no way to gauge my progress. As I crawled, I swept my hands in a semi-circle in front of me, the sound of my breath unnaturally loud in my ears, my eyes straining in vain.

As a child, I was never afraid of the dark, but I had never been in such unremitting darkness before. There was nothing. Just complete and total obscurity. It was unnerving, I couldn't seem to get my bearings. I had to keep telling myself to move because everything inside of me wanted to curl up into a ball and hide until this was over. "Don't stop," I whispered to myself. "Don't stop."

After what seemed like a very long time, though it was

probably no more than ten minutes, I touched smooth plastic.

"I found it!" I cried out, exulting in my small success. "Harry, I found it!"

"That is good."

I grabbed hold of the ice chest, pulling it close and wrapping my arms around it. As I lay my head on top of it, tears of relief pricked my eyelids. I felt as if I had been rescued. I was no longer drifting in an empty, black sea of nothingness. I had found a lifebuoy, a lifebuoy in the shape of a small cooler.

I'm not sure how long I lay in the darkness clinging to the ice chest, but it was a while before I felt secure enough to loosen my grip and search for the latch. My knees, scraped and raw from my crawl across the floor, stung painfully as I knelt on the cold, rough bricks. I ran my fingers over it and found the latch, then opened the cooler.

"There's a blanket inside," I called out to Harry. I pulled out the blanket and felt underneath. Plastic bottles and a couple of plastic containers were stacked inside. "And some bottles and maybe some food. I'm not sure," I said, my fingers grazing the tops of two containers.

"Food and drink. Good. You need to eat and drink now."

I sat down on the floor, draping it over my shoulders like a cape. It wasn't much, but I was grateful for the little warmth it provided. Reaching into the cooler, I pulled out one of the bottles. For a moment, I thought about not drinking anything, afraid that it might be drugged, but my thirst got the better of me. I had no idea how long I was going to be here, and Harry was right; I need to eat and drink to keep up my strength.

I opened a bottle and drank greedily.

CHAPTER 12

A GHOST AMONG THE LIVING

1943
Late Summer

For two days, with little food and water, sleeping only in brief snatches, he rowed. Muscles seizing and cramping, he rowed. With raw, bloody hands slipping and sliding on the wooden oars, he rowed. He rowed and rowed and rowed. When he finally sighted land, Heinrich would have wept tears of joy if he had been able to. He had done it! He had survived! He had rowed across the English Channel!

The bottom of his waterlogged boat scraped along rocks and sand as he neared the beach and Heinrich tumbled out onto the shore more dead than alive. He stumbled along the beach until he came across an abandoned fishing shed. He crawled inside. Overcome with physical exhaustion, he promptly fell into a deep, dreamless sleep.

It was dark when he awoke. His first sensation was that of a desperate, ravenous thirst. He ran his tongue over his swollen, cracked lips and swallowed or tried to swallow. His mouth and throat felt as if they had been scraped raw. Water. He needed water.

Driven by a pressing thirst, he walked into the village. When he saw the garden hose in the side garden of the small cottage, he almost cried out with relief. He fell on the hose, drinking greedily, heedless of the risk of waking the inhabitants. Nearby a dog began barking. Its owner grumpily shouted at it to be quiet as Heinrich hurried along the road. He had no idea where he was or in which direction London lay, but he walked anyway, trusting that he would eventually find his way to London.

He traveled at night. It was easier that way. Traveling during daylight was too risky. He attracted too much attention from the English villagers who stared and gawked at him as he walked along the roads.

The first time it happened, he'd broken out in a cold sweat, his heart racing violently as he waited for someone to denounce him as a German spy. When no one began shouting, he'd forced himself to keep walking calmly, nodding pleasantly to the women, the children, and the old people as they gawked. It wasn't until later that he realized that the villagers weren't staring at him because he was foreign. They were staring at him because he was an able-bodied man, all the other men having left the villages to fight the war.

Traveling at night also made it easier for him to fend for himself. While the inhabitants of the small coastal villages slumbered, he helped himself to the vegetables in their gardens, the eggs in their hen houses, and the milk bottles left on their doorsteps. He clothed himself with items he found hanging from clotheslines. When he was fortunate enough to find a newspaper in the rubbish, he practiced reading it aloud to improve his English. During the day, he took shelter where he could find it.

As the weeks passed and the weather became increasingly colder and wetter, he often spent his days curled under shrubs or trees, shivering beneath a stolen blanket as he waited for the sun to set so he could continue on his way. It was a long, miserable walk, but it gave him time to heal and learn about the English and their customs. It took him more than a month, but by the time he finally arrived in London, people no longer stared at him. He was one of many men in the city. True, most wore uniforms, but not all of them, and so no one paid much attention to him.

His first impression of London was one of absolute shock at the devastation the German bombs had wrought on the city. People had made an effort to clean the streets, but there was no hiding the crumbled bricks and burnt timbers that littered the yards of damaged homes and buildings. In some areas, entire blocks had been reduced to rubble and had been abandoned. Other neighborhoods looked as if they had escaped the bombings unscathed. It wasn't unusual to see a home with a caved-in roof standing next to another house that was completely undamaged. Once he stumbled across a house that looked as if it had been sliced in half with a knife. Half of the house had been obliterated while the other half stood untouched. The upstairs rooms opened to the air like a giant dollhouse, bed frames and wardrobes still in place, curtains flapping in the breeze.

Heinrich quickly realized that the German bombs that had destroyed many of the buildings in the city worked to his advantage, providing him with any number of broken and abandoned shelters. He found plenty of abandoned buildings that kept him relatively dry if not especially warm.

Making sure to change his location every few days, in order to avoid the Civil Defense guards, he spent his time reading discarded newspapers, listening and practicing his English. Heinrich ventured out on the streets only at night where he could hide his foreignness under the protective cloak of darkness.

Because of the blackout, London was plunged into almost absolute darkness as soon as night fell. Streetlights, which would have normally illuminated roads and walkways, were switched off. Thick black curtains covered building windows to prevent even the faintest light from escaping. Even automobile headlights were dimmed or masked with black material. All of this was done to make it difficult for the German bombers to find the city. Heinrich wasn't convinced it deterred the *Luftwaffe* with their sophisticated airplanes, but it did protect him. Sometimes as he sauntered unseen past the shuttered silhouettes of the houses, listening to strains of music or bits of conversation wafting through the dark streets, he felt like a ghost walking among the living.

CHAPTER 13

A SISTER CALLS

December 8
1:45 a.m.

The sound of his mobile woke him. Simon grabbed it and eyed the screen. Thought briefly about letting it go to message, but knowing how determined his sister was, decided that it would be best to get it over with.

"Hullo."

"What is going on!" Jenna demanded. Not bothering to greet him. "First, you ring me up asking if I know where Lily is. Then Mum calls asking the same question. I've rung Lily twenty times and every time it goes straight to voicemail."

Simon sat up, raking his fingers through his hair. "Umm, Jenna, do you know what time it is? It's almost two in the morning!"

"Of course, I bloody well know what time it is! Tell me what is going on! Why isn't Lily answering her phone, and why is everyone calling me to find out where she is!"

Simon sighed heavily. His sister was like a bulldog. Once she got something in her teeth, she didn't let go until she had finished gnawing it to death.

"She's gone missing."

"What! She's gone missing? What is that supposed to mean?"

"It means that she's gone missing. She's not at her flat and she's not answering her phone."

"People just don't go missing, Simon. That's daft." She paused. "Oh, no! Do you think she was in an accident? Did you check the hospitals?"

"I'm sure the police are doing that."

"How do you know?"

"They're the police. They know how to look for missing people."

"Have you talked to any of her mates from university?"

"Jenna," he said, trying to be patient. "The police are investigating."

"The police are investigating," she repeated snarkily. "Simon, what are you doing to find her?"

"I'm …" He paused. "I'm doing what I can."

"Which is what?"

"Jenna, the police are investigating."

"I'm coming to London."

"No. No, you're not."

"Simon Fitzgibbon, don't you tell me what I am going to do or not do!"

Simon tried acting like the reasonable older brother. The last thing he needed was for Jenna to come to London and start questioning people. Inspector Shah had made it quite clear that it was in Lily's best interest that they avoid publicity about the kidnapping and ransom. "Look, Jenna. Coming to London isn't going to help Lily or you. You need to study for your exams. The police are doing everything they can to find her. You aren't going to be able to do anything more than they are."

"What about Ben? Did anyone ask Ben? Maybe he knows something."

Simon gritted his teeth. "No. No one asked Ben."

"The police should ring Ben," Jenna insisted.

"Why should they ring Ben?" Simon asked, carefully.

Jenna must have heard it anyway, the small twinge of jealousy that infused his voice. "Because he and Lily are friends. That's why. That whole bit about last summer, that wasn't really Lily. You know that."

Simon didn't bother to reply. The events of last summer still rankled, even though he knew it was neither Lily nor Ben's fault.

"Look, Simon, Lily and Ben are friends. I know that they've met for coffee a couple of times. You should call him. Perhaps she said something to him."

"You ring Ben," he snapped. "I'm going back to sleep."

"Fine. I'll do that," she replied tartly, ending the call abruptly.

But he didn't go back to sleep. Jenna's words kept echoing in his head. *"What are you doing to find her?"*

CHAPTER 14

RACHEL

1943
Fall

After three weeks in London, Heinrich had become familiar with the city. He learned which streets he should avoid (Civil Defense patrols and American soldiers tended to stick to the main roads) and where to scavenge food (expensive hotels and bakeries discarded the best scraps).

One night, as he walked along a service road, he heard a young woman's angry voice coming from a nearby alleyway.

"Take your hands off me!"

Heinrich paused.

"Just being friendly." The slurred voice of a drunk man retorted. "How 'bout it, sweetheart?"

"Take your hands off me at once!"

A very proper, very angry English woman confronted by a very drunk American soldier, Heinrich thought as he listened to the exchange.

"Yer a feisty little thing."

"Stop that!"

"Oh, no you don't." The drunk's voice rose.

The girl gasped.

A second voice spoke. "Whatcher got there, Pete?"

"Found us a live one."

"Let go of me," the girl cried out. "You're hurting me!"

Heinrich stepped into the alley. In the darkness, he could just make out the silhouettes of two men. They had pinned the girl against the brick wall, laughing as she struggled to free herself.

Without thinking, Heinrich shouted at the two soldiers. "Halt!"

The two men paused and looked up.

"You will halt!" Heinrich ordered loudly.

The first man spoke up. "Did you hear that? He sounds like a Kraut."

"He ain't no Limey that's fer sure," the second one agreed.

"You will halt!" Heinrich repeated.

"London ain't no place for a Kraut. At least not one that ain't dead already." The bulkier of the two men straightened up. "You keep hold of the girl. I'll take care of the Kraut," he told his friend.

He lurched toward Heinrich, who ducked the first blow. Heinrich dropped his shoulders and hit the American low. The American soldier was drunk, and his reflexes were slow, but he was still strong. The two of them grappled, landing punches and kicks until Heinrich finally managed to land a fist on the man's jaw. As the man crumpled to the ground, his friend let go of the girl and charged Heinrich. "You filthy Kraut," he bellowed.

Heinrich easily side-stepped the soldier, taking only a glancing blow. Off balance, the American crashed head-first into the side of a building and slid to the ground, where he stayed. Heinrich straightened up, breathing heavily.

He heard sirens. Belatedly, he realized that his good deed may have cost him his life. To his great surprise, the English girl hadn't run away.

She grabbed his hand. "This way," she whispered. "Follow me."

They ran through an alley and exited onto a different street. She slowed her pace to a quick walk. "Don't run," she said. "Someone will notice."

She linked her arm through his. "This way. Come with me."

They walked without speaking until they came to an apartment building. Pulling a key out of her purse with a trembling hand, she opened the front door. She held a finger to her lips and pointed up the stairs, indicating that he should follow her quietly.

Heinrich tiptoed up the stairway, listening as police sirens sounded in the distance.

The girl ushered him inside her flat and closed the door quickly behind him. He stood uncertainly and watched as she pulled black heavy curtains across the windows. Only when the windows were completely covered did she turn on a small table lamp.

Heinrich stared at her. She was small and slender with thick dark hair and wide brown eyes. She was wearing a nurse's uniform.

"You're hurt," she said, examining him critically. "Sit down. Over there." She pointed to a small table with two chairs. "I'll get a towel and some water."

Thinking to himself that this was a woman used to giving orders, Heinrich silently obeyed. Her touch was gentle. Still, he winced as she cleaned his cuts and bruises.

"Thank you," she said to him. "For coming to my rescue. I shouldn't have taken that alley. I know better, but I was in a hurry to get home and, well …" She paused. "I'm sorry you were hurt, but I am very glad you were there."

Heinrich said nothing, waiting stoically until she had

finished.

"There, that's better," she said, surveying her work.

Heinrich stood. "Thank you," he said formally. "I am happy you are not hurt."

She smiled up at him. "Please sit down. I'll make us some tea. It's the least I can do," she offered.

"I must go."

"Have you eaten?"

Seeing the indecision in Heinrich's eyes, she pressed her advantage. "Please stay. It will give me a chance to repay you for your help. I'll make us something to eat. It won't be much, but it will be hot."

It caught him by surprise, the sudden terrible, aching loneliness. It was almost a physical need, like hunger or thirst, a primal longing to be recognized as a member of the human race. Heinrich knew he should go. It was dangerous for him to be here, but it had been so long since he had human company.

Overcome with the emotion, he was unable to speak. He nodded.

"Good, that's settled then."

The smile she gave him was as dazzling as the sun reflecting on newly fallen snow. It was bright and warm and welcoming. For a moment, his longing for human companionship was so intense that he closed his eyes.

"Since you're staying for dinner, I suppose we should introduce ourselves. My name is Rachel."

"Harry," Heinrich said, translating his German name into English. "My name is Harry."

"It is very nice to meet you, Harry," she said, gracing him with another smile.

"I too am pleased to make your acquaintance, Rachel," he said, clicking his heels together and acknowledging her with a gentlemanly bow.

She looked surprised at his formal gesture. Her delighted laugh had an almost musical quality to it. For the first time in a long time, Heinrich found himself laughing, too. *I will remember this night as the best night of my life*, he thought to himself.

They ate by the light of the one lamp. She made scrambled eggs and served them with some kind of tinned meat. She did most of the talking, but Heinrich enjoyed her chatter. She was a nurse. She had been returning from her shift at the hospital when the two soldiers accosted her on the street. He felt himself relaxing as she talked. It was as if he were coming back from the dead. He was no longer a walking ghost. Tonight, he was human again.

After dinner, she stood and leaned forward, reaching to remove the dishes from the table. The collar of her blouse fell open. For the first time Heinrich noticed the necklace she wore around her neck. He froze, his eyes glued on the gold Star of David.

She noticed his stare and with a small apologetic smile, tucked the necklace inside her blouse again.

"You are Jewish," Heinrich said in shocked surprise.

"Yes," she replied and her eyes locked onto his. "Are you?" she asked.

"I must go." He stood abruptly. "I thank you for the food and for the …" He touched the gash on his forehead.

"And where will you go?" she said, eyebrows raised. It was a statement more than a question. "Do you have papers?"

Heinrich didn't answer. She knew. How?

As if he had asked the question aloud, she answered. "Someone who had nothing to fear from the police would not have run. Your clothes." She shrugged apologetically. "You've been sleeping rough."

Heinrich looked down at his stolen clothes self-consciously. Suddenly embarrassed, he realized how filthy he was. "I do not have papers."

"Are you a refugee?"

"I left the war," he said simply.

Rachel's eyes were sympathetic. "If the American soldiers tell them about the German who assaulted them, the police will be looking for you. If the soldiers find you, they will put you in prison or shoot you," she said matter-of-factly.

Heinrich's eyes widened. "You know I am German? You invited a German into your home?"

She held his gaze. "There are good and bad people everywhere, Harry. I know you are a good man." She cleared the dishes. "Why don't you help me wash up? You may sleep on the sofa tonight."

CHAPTER 15

OFFICIALLY MISSING

December 8
11:00 a.m.

David Deene's face flushed. His jaw popped and flexed angrily.

Simon glanced at Lily's mother. She leaned against Lord Yarlbury, dark half-moon bruises shadowed her eyes.

"I'm sorry, Maggie," David Deene said, not quite managing to sound contrite. His gaze flicked over Inspector Shah and Lord Yarlbury. He ignored Simon. "I'm worried about Lily and I let it get to me."

"We're all worried about Lily," Lord Yarlbury said, fixing David Deene with a level gaze. "However, that does not give you a license to shout."

"Please," Lady Yarlbury interjected softly. "This is hard enough as it is. Let's not make it any more difficult."

Lord Yarlbury looked at her with concern, patting her arm gently.

Inspector Shah cleared his throat. "Perhaps we should begin."

They had reached the magical number of twenty-four hours; Lily was now considered officially missing by the Metropolitan Police. Inspector Shah had arranged a meeting with David Deene and Lord and Lady Yarlbury.

Inspector Shah began speaking. Simon's exhaustion and anxiety left him feeling restless and unsettled. Unable to decide where to sit, he chose to stand.

He had slept very little between Jenna's phone call and thoughts of Lily cannoning around his head: Lily afraid, Lily alone, Lily hurt. Worrying about her had kept him awake and he spent most of the night tossing and turning on his mate's sofa. When exhaustion had finally overtaken him, his dreams had been filled with those same haunting images until he jerked awake, his heart lurching in his chest, his skin damp with sweat.

As Shah began his preliminary questions, Simon leaned against the doorframe and observed the others. Lord and Lady Yarlbury sat next to each other on the sofa. Lily's American father and Inspector Shah sat opposite them in matching chairs. Lily's mother looked as if she had been hollowed out from the inside and might crumble at any moment. Lord Yarlbury looked tired and tense, but resolute. David Deene was angry and confrontational.

Of the four people sitting in the living room, only Shah appeared to be untouched by the situation. He spoke with a calm confidence and authority that was meant to reassure, but only increased the tension in the room.

"Is anything else missing from the flat?" Inspector Shah asked.

Lord Yarlbury shook his head. "As far as we know, nothing is missing."

Simon rested the back of his head against the wall and sent out a silent prayer to Lily. "Be safe. Be strong," he pleaded silently.

Inspector Shah continued directing his questions to

Lord and Lady Yarlbury. "Were you able to locate her keys?" he asked.

Lady Yarlbury shook her head, her mouth trembling with emotion. She leaned against Lord Yarlbury, taking her strength from him.

"No," his lordship answered for her. "The spare keys are here, but her set of keys is missing."

Shah turned to look at Deene. "The doorman said that you met your daughter outside the building. She had returned from shopping. Is that correct?"

"Yes."

"Did she use keys to let herself into the flat?"

"Yes."

"Where did she keep her keys?"

"In her purse."

Did you happen to look at her keys? Perhaps you noticed her key fob?"

David Deene exhaled angrily. "She took the keys out of her purse. That's all I noticed. Why are we going on and on about her keys? My daughter has been abducted! You need to be looking for her, not looking for her damn keys!"

Inspector Shah smiled sympathetically. His voice was gentle. "Mr. Deene, I understand that you are anxious to find your daughter. We all are. However, before we can begin any search, we need to understand how this situation might have come about. There was no forced entry into the flat. At this point, we are trying to determine if your daughter was abducted in this building or at some other location. Perhaps the person or persons who abducted her were known to her. She may have loaned them her keys. She may have let them into her flat, or she may have left the flat to meet them somewhere else. At this point, we have no idea how this person or persons entered the building. When we understand how your daughter was abducted, we will be that much closer to finding her. I understand you may be frustrated, but I assure you that things will go better if we make sure we have all of the facts of the situation."

David Deene leaned forward in his chair, his breathing rapid, his face flushed. He jabbed his finger accusingly at the police inspector. "This is not a situation! My daughter has been abducted by a criminal! I don't need you to patronize me. I don't need to be schooled in police procedure! I need you to find my daughter! I need you to *do your job*!"

"David, stop being such an ass."

Everyone looked at Lady Yarlbury in shocked surprise.

"Sit down and answer the inspector's questions." Her voice was quiet yet forceful. "Lily is missing. This is not about you. This is about Lily. You will help me find her. We are going to do whatever it takes to find our daughter. Right now, that means that you are going to sit down and answer the inspector's questions."

David Deene's face darkened and something flickered in his eyes. Anger? Resentment? Respect? Simon couldn't quite decide what it was.

"All right, Maggie," Lily's father said with a grudging nod in Lady Yarlbury's direction. "We'll do it your way. For now. But if I don't see any results, then I'm going to do it my way." He shot another dark look in Lord Yarlbury's direction before lowering himself into the chair.

Simon watched the scene unfold with a mixture of disbelief and surprise. Perhaps he shouldn't have been surprised. Lady Yarlbury was a mother, a mother fiercely protecting her child, even if that meant standing up to a bullying ex-husband.

David Deene, on the other hand, was a puzzle. Based on what Lily had shared with him, Simon knew David Deene would never be a contender for "Father of the Year." Yet, he appeared to be truly undone by everything that had happened.

Though, Simon couldn't help but feel that there was something off about his anger and outrage. Of course,

Simon had to admit, he didn't really know the man. Perhaps belligerence and bullying were simply normal, everyday behavior for him. That might explain his angry outbursts. It didn't explain, however, why a father who hadn't bothered to see or speak to his daughter for years suddenly showed up in London the day before she suddenly went missing.

CHAPTER 16

LOST

December 8
11:00 a.m.

It's funny how the importance of an object can change depending upon the circumstances. A little plastic box. That's all it was, nothing more than a cooler that you would never think twice about unless you were going on a picnic or to the beach. And yet, this small box had become incredibly important to me. I clung to the cooler as if my life depended upon it.

Logically I knew that the small chest wasn't going anywhere. But somewhere deep inside of me was this fear that if I let go of it, I would be swept away into the vast ocean of nothingness that surrounded me. So, I held onto it, wrapping my hand tightly around the handle, even as I curled up on the floor and closed my eyes as the darkness crashed over me in waves.

I awoke, confused and disoriented. It took a moment

before I remembered where I was. I sat up stiff with cold, my left arm numb, feeling anxious and unsettled. Without any light, I had no way of judging how long I'd been sleeping or even how long I had been here.

I scooted closer to the ice chest and rested my leg against it, rubbing my now tingling arm. As I did, I thought I heard something. I stilled, listening. Was I imagining it? I wasn't sure.

I was struck by a sudden thought. If I could hear them, maybe they could hear me.

"HELP!" I screamed wildly, my voice echoing weirdly. "HELP! HELP ME! I NEED HELP! PLEASE HELP ME!"

I yelled until I had to pause and catch my breath.

"They cannot hear you."

"Harry?"

"They cannot hear you when you shout. The walls, they are too thick."

I closed my eyes, too tired and defeated to even cry.

I sat in the silence, oblivious to everything except my own misery. Until I became aware of something else, something I couldn't ignore. I had to pee. Badly. Was there a bathroom in this place? Probably not, but even if there was, how could I possibly find it? I looked around, blinking blindly as I squirmed. I was going to have to do something soon or I was going to be in trouble.

"There is a pail," Harry said to me as if we were in the middle of a conversation.

"A pail?"

"So you can ..." He cleared his throat. "Relieve yourself."

"Relieve myself?" A light bulb went off in my head. "Oh."

"Do you know where it is?" I asked, turning blindly toward his voice.

"It is near, I think."

Keeping one hand on the ice chest, I stretched out and

felt around in the dark, patting the floor near me. I didn't find anything. The rational part of me knew that I was going to have to let go of the ice chest, but I was so afraid of being cast adrift in the dark that I held on with one hand and stretched my arms out as far as I could to continue my search. When that failed, I stretched my legs out in front of me.

"I can't find it."

"It is near."

I lay down on the floor, still holding onto the handle of the ice chest and stretched out. Pointing my toes to extend my reach, I swept my legs across the floor.

The tip of my toe caught something, knocking it over. I heard the clunk of the metal against the bricks as the pail I so desperately needed rolled away from me. I swore, and tears of frustration filled my eyes.

I had a choice. I could let go of the cooler and find the pail, or I could … well, it really wasn't a choice. I inhaled deeply and let go, frantically scrabbling across the floor as I searched for the bucket. The blackness swelled and rolled around me in disorienting waves. When my fingers came into contact with cold metal, I almost sobbed with relief. I grasped the handle of the pail and crawling on all fours, managed to drag it back in the direction of the ice chest, my head spinning with the effort.

When I arrived at the place where I thought the icebox should be, I felt a momentary jolt of panic when it wasn't there. Fear shooting through me, I swung the bucket in a wide arc in front of me hoping to find it. Inching forward I kept swinging the bucket until it thudded against plastic. Chest heaving, I threw myself at the cooler and grabbed onto it like a life buoy.

My fear and desperation momentarily distracted me from my pressing need to pee. I had to wait until my heart rate slowed before taking care of my business with the bucket.

My face burning with humiliation, I attempted to, as

Harry so delicately put it, relieve myself. I had no other choice. I knew Harry couldn't see me, but there was nothing I could do about the noise. Harry was tactfully silent. When I finished, I pushed the bucket far enough away from me so that I wouldn't accidentally knock it over, then pulled the woolen blanket over my shoulders and huddled next to the cooler.

I closed my eyes. It seemed to make the immense emptiness surrounding me less frightening. The air was damp and smelled of mildew. The cold seeped through the blanket and into my bones. I brushed the ice chest with the back of my hand, reassuring myself that it was there.

"Harry?" I called.

"*Ja.* Yes," he answered.

"Do you think he's called my mother? For the money, I mean?"

"I do not know this."

"He must have called her." I sighed and pulled the blanket more tightly around my shoulders, shivering. "She is going to be so worried about me. And Simon. Oh God! Simon is probably at the apartment right now, wondering where I am." Tears welled up in my eyes. I squeezed my eyes closed to keep the tears from falling. Crying wasn't going to help me.

"You must be strong. You must have …" Harry paused. "Courage. You must have courage."

"What if they don't let me go?" I asked, my voice faltering.

"You will go when they have the money." His voice sounded tired.

My conscience pricked at me. I was feeling so sorry for myself that I hadn't thought much about Harry. He probably had family who was worried about him, too.

"Harry, how long have you been here?" I asked.

He was quiet for a moment, thinking. "A long time, I think."

A hot, hard lump formed in my throat. "Oh, Harry.

CHAPTER 17

PICKLES AND EGGS

1943
Late Fall

The first time Rachael lit the candles, Heinrich had been both apprehensive and intrigued. She had draped a shawl over her hair and shoulders, explaining the ritual to him as she carefully placed two candles on the kitchen table.

"We put the candles on the table to remember and to celebrate the Sabbath. It is a day of rest, so we take time to remind ourselves to keep true to his commandments. For us, Shabbat begins on sunset Friday and continues until sunset on Saturday." She'd looked up and had given him a quick, warm smile. "But I expect you know that already." Her smile held no judgment, and for that, Heinrich had been grateful.

She lit the candles and waved her hands gracefully over them three times before covering her eyes and reciting a prayer. She had translated the prayer for him:

Baruch atah Adonai, Eloheinu, melech ha'olam,
Blessed are you, Lord, our God, Sovereign of the universe,
asher kidishanu b'mitz'votav v'tzivanu …
who has sanctified us with commandments and commanded us …
l'had'lik ner shel Shabbat.
to kindle the light of Shabbat.

He had been surprised to find that the prayer she recited wasn't all that different from some of the prayers he had learned as a boy. How was it possible that he had not known that Jews and Christians worshiped the same God?

Tonight, when Rachel finished the prayer, she opened her eyes and smiled at him. "You are listening very intently tonight."

"Your eyes are closed. How do you know that I am listening and not stealing your bread?" Heinrich teased her.

"I could feel you staring at me," she told him. "What is wrong?"

The shawl she used to cover her hair framed her face with its soft folds of fabric. In the candlelight she looked radiant, her skin almost luminescent. She looked, he thought, like an angel. Did Jews believe in angels? He didn't know, but then he realized it didn't matter because he believed in angels. How could he not believe in angels when he was sitting at a table staring at the most beautiful angel he had ever seen.

For almost two weeks, Rachel had sheltered him in her flat, asking for nothing in return. He was grateful for her kindness, but he knew the time was coming for him to leave. Every day that he stayed, he placed her at risk. If the police found him, or if someone reported him to the proper authorities, Rachel would be accused of sheltering an enemy combatant. It would mean jail or worse for her.

"Rachel," he said sadly. "I must leave here. It is not good for you that I stay here."

"And if you leave, where will you go?" she asked.

He shrugged.

"If the police or someone finds you, what will you do?"

He shrugged again.

Her eyebrows drew together, forming a small crease in the middle of her forehead. "If they find you, they will think you are a German spy and you will get shot." Her gentle brown eyes held his gaze. "You must stay here." She removed the shawl from her hair and sat down.

"Rachel …" he began.

Before he could finish what he was saying, she reached across the kitchen table and placed her small hand on top of his. "Too many good men have died in this war, Harry. You must stay here."

"Your neighbors will think—"

"I will tell the neighbors that you are my cousin," she interrupted. "And that you are suffering from shell shock, that crowds and loud noises upset you, so you do not go out until after dark. They won't ask any questions," she assured him. "But you mustn't speak to any of the neighbors. You don't sound like an Englishman. Not yet," she said with a gentle teasing smile. "You will be safe here. Stay here and practice your English. When the war is over, we will find your mother's people."

Coward that he was, he agreed.

Heinrich, wanting desperately to do something to repay the kindness Rachel had shown him, insisted on escorting her to and from her shift at the hospital. Each evening he accompanied Rachael to and from the heavy iron gates that marked the entrance of the hospital. It was a small thing, but at least he felt as if he was doing something useful and helping to keep her safe. He always waited until she had safely entered before wandering the unlit streets of London, searching for ways to supplement their meager larder.

Food and milk were in such short supply in the city that they could only be purchased with ration coupons issued by the English government. Rachael's ration coupons were enough to feed one person, now she was feeding two. She had traded her unused bacon coupons with a Christian neighbor for extra cheese and dried eggs, but the food was not nearly enough to feed both of them. So after Rachel went to work, Heinrich scavenged the vacant bomb-damaged buildings and empty market stalls for anything they might be able to eat.

One night while he was walking near the Savoy Hotel, a man's voice hailed Heinrich.

"Watcher, Mate! 'Old up."

Heinrich paused, his heart thumping painfully in his chest. Fearing the worst, he'd slowly turned to face the man. Even in the dim moonlight, Heinrich could see that the man wasn't wearing a police uniform.

Relieved, he asked, "Me?" He kept his voice low and raspy to hide his German accent.

"You look to be a strong enough blighter. Got both your legs and arms, don'tcha? 'Ow 'bout 'elping me out. I've got a delivery." The small man had jerked his thumb at the hotel building. "Lorry's parked out back."

Heinrich had eyed the man suspiciously. He was small, but that hadn't meant he didn't have a partner skulking around the back ready to rob him. Not that Heinrich had had anything worth taking, but that man wouldn't know that. He'd stared at the man for a long moment, appraising him.

"All right then, suit yerself, mate," the man had said when Heinrich didn't answer. He turned away and began walking toward the hotel. Heinrich had noticed that the man walked with a pronounced limp.

Heinrich waited until the man had disappeared around the corner of the building before cautiously following him.

The man had been telling the truth. There had been a

lorry parked at the service entrance of the hotel. A lorry filled with food! Heinrich hadn't seen that much food in years. Crates of eggs, cheese, chicken, and vegetables had filled the back of the truck.

Heinrich had cautiously approached the truck. The man had been busying stacking crates on the ground. Heinrich cleared his throat and the man looked up.

"Changed yer mind? Good. I can use the 'elp. I can't pay, but I can set aside a bit of the merchandise after we get 'er unloaded. They keep accounts, but there's always a few things that fall off the truck, if you get my meaning. That's better than a few bob, I say," he continued. "No sense in 'aving money when you can't find nothing to buy. Right?" The man had held out his hand. "Name's Jack. Jack Daw."

Heinrich shook it. "Harry," he'd answered in the same low raspy voice.

"All right, 'Arry. Let's get to work."

Jack then handed Heinrich a box filled with carrots, jars of pickles and, most amazing of all, plucked chickens.

Heinrich had stared open-mouthed at the food.

Jack nodded. "More where that come from. I make the rounds. The Savoy, the Grosvenor, the Goring, the Claridge, and the Ritz. The toffs and military big brass are staying in the 'otels. Closed up them big 'ouses they did. No servants to be 'ad. Don't need ration cards, do they? Government says they got to be fed. I deliver the food to the 'otels. Not a bad job. 'As got its benefits," he'd said, pointing to the open door at the back of the hotel. "Just put it on the counter."

Heinrich had helped Jack unload the rest of the food. When they'd finished, Jack handed Heinrich a jar of pickles and six eggs.

"Yer a 'ard worker, 'Arry. Don't talk too much. I like that. With my bum leg, I could use a 'elping 'and. I'm at the Grosvenor on Wednesday. If yer interested."

Heinrich nodded. "I will be there."

He had found his first job in England.

CHAPTER 18

FOUND

December 8
5:00 p.m.

My thoughts were becoming clearer and more focused. I'd been drugged, but I was feeling better now. The nausea and confusion were finally gone. Harry had been right. The food and water helped.

I took stock of the contents of the cooler. I had four bottles of water and one cheese sandwich remaining. It wasn't much, which meant that the man who'd left the cooler would probably be returning soon.

I pulled the blanket tightly around my shoulders. I thought of Simon and my mother and my baby brother, Will. I couldn't just give up. I had to do something. I couldn't just keep waiting for the man in the mask to come back.

"Harry, I need to find a way out of here."

CHAPTER 19

THE RANSOM

December 8
5:00 p.m.

Lord Yarlbury's mobile phone sounded. He glanced down at it, his eyes flickering in the direction of Inspector Shah and a uniformed police officer whom Shah introduced as Sergeant Fis. "I don't recognize the number."

"Can you record the call?" Shah asked.

Lord Yarlbury nodded.

"Record the call. If it is our man, we can play it back."

His lordship answered the phone and Simon knew from the expression on his face that the call was from the person who had taken Lily.

Lord Yarlbury listened without speaking for a few moments.

"I might need another day to make the financial arrangements," he said, his voice noticeably tight with anger. A muscle jumped in his jaw as he listened to the caller, but he remained silent.

"I understand," Lord Yarlbury replied. He waited a moment, then hit the end button, terminating the call. He looked up, his eyes skimming across each of them. "It was he," Lord Yarlbury said unnecessarily.

"Were you able to record the call?" Shah asked.

Lord Yarlbury glanced down at his mobile before answering. "Yes," then placed it in the middle of the table and played the recording.

Simon moved closer to the table. His eyes locked on the device as a male voice started speaking. The voice of the caller was raspy, as if he were trying to disguise it.

"We got a business proposition for your *lordship*," the voice sneered. "You want your stepdaughter and we want what's owed us. You pay five hundred thousand quid and we give you the girl. We're not greedy, we're only collecting what's owed. Five hundred thousand pounds and the girl goes home."

The recording of Lord Yarlbury's voice echoed strangely. "I might need another day to make financial arrangements."

"Don't try that with me," the voice barked angrily. "Toffs like you always know how to get your hands on dosh. You get it or the girl won't be going back to the old pile, now will she? I'll ring you and tell you where to bring it. Oh. And another thing. You bring the police and our business deal is off. You got that? All we want to see is you and the dosh. No police! You bring the cozzers and the girl dies! You don't pay the money and the girl dies! You got that?"

"I understand."

The call ended.

Simon stepped back, away from the table, as he fought to control the rage and fear that burned in his gut. He wanted to make that sneering voice pay for what he'd done to Lily! He wanted to pound the man to a bloody pulp with his bare hands. He stood, fists clenched at his sides, breathing heavily, shaking with emotion.

Inspector Shah was the first to speak. His voice was calm and controlled. "Does anyone recognize the voice?" he asked, glancing at each of them in turn. No one answered.

"I don't understand. What does he mean that we owe him money?" Lady Yarlbury asked, looking at her husband uncertainly.

"I haven't the faintest idea."

Simon could see it in her eyes, in the way she looked at Lord Yarlbury, that she wasn't sure if he was telling the truth.

"But, Richard, why would he say that? Why would he say we owe him money if we don't?"

"I don't know. All I know is we don't owe anyone money."

"But why would he think that? Why would he think we owe him money?"

"It doesn't matter who owes the money," David Deene interjected. He had been unusually silent up until this point in their meeting. "You need to pay the ransom." His eyes ricocheted around the table. "You heard what he said. If you don't pay it, he'll kill her."

"That is not something I would recommend, at this juncture," Inspector Shah said.

David Deene whipped around to stare at the police inspector. "What do you mean you don't recommend it? We pay him! We have to pay him!" His voice had a desperate edge to it.

"There are certain protocols we can use to negotiate her safe return. Paying the ransom …"

"Negotiate? You want to negotiate? This is my daughter we're talking about!" Deene's voice shook. "We pay him exactly what he wants, when he wants it. There is no negotiating! We do exactly what he says! You heard what he said. If we don't pay, he will kill her!"

For the first time, Simon found himself in agreement with Lily's father. He would do anything to get Lily back safely.

"Yes. This is your daughter we are talking about," Inspector Shah agreed. He looked at each of them in turn, including Simon with a flick of a glance in his direction. "However, as of right now, you have no way of verifying that the person who called with the ransom demand is the same person who has taken Lily." He paused. "Or that Lily is alive."

A small strangled sound escaped from the back of Lady Yarlbury's throat.

Shah eyed her sympathetically. "I apologize. I know that is difficult to hear, but it is a fact. In these situations, the people you are dealing with are not honorable. If you give in to their demands without our help, there exists the possibility that the people who did this will take the money and not release your daughter." He turned and fixed his gaze on Lord Yarlbury. "We have protocols for this type of thing. Before you pay any ransom, we need to establish contact with the captors to negotiate with them. Before we go any further, we need proof of her well-being. When he calls again, you need to demand proof that Lily is alive."

Lady Yarlbury gasped and covered her mouth with trembling hands.

David Deene's eyes flashed defiantly, although Simon could sense fear lurking behind his anger. "I don't care what the hell your protocols say. These people mean business! We don't negotiate! Not with my daughter's life at risk! The man said five hundred thousand pounds. It doesn't matter who owes the money! We do exactly what he says. We pay the ransom! Without the police!" He turned to look at Lady Yarlbury, his voice softening. "Maggie, we can't take the chance that they might hurt her."

"Mr. Deene," Inspector Shah interjected. "Having a missing child is an extremely difficult situation. I understand your concerns. We have experience—"

David Deene cut him off, jabbing his finger angrily in the air. "No!" He leaped to his feet. "We need to do exactly what they want! I won't allow you to put her life in jeopardy!"

Inspector Shah's eyes locked onto Lily's father. "Mr. Deene," he replied, his voice hard and flat. "I am here to ensure the safe return of your daughter. The best way to accomplish that is to permit me to do my job."

"David, I think we should listen to what the inspector has to say," Lily's mom said quietly.

"You, too, Maggie?" He narrowed his eyes and looked accusingly at Lily's mother. "Is it the money? Are you really going to let him risk our daughter's life for money?"

Lady Yarlbury closed her eyes as if she was in pain. "David, the police have experience with these sorts of things. I think we should do what they say."

David Deene leaped to his feet, his face red with fury. "Don't you think our daughter's life is worth five hundred thousand pounds? Five hundred thousand pounds is nothing to him," he shouted, pointing a finger at Lord Yarlbury. "But it could mean Lily's life. Are you willing to let him negotiate for our daughter? How much? How much is her life worth to you, Maggie? How much? Two hundred thousand? Fifty thousand? What price are you willing to pay for your daughter?"

Lord Yarlbury's expression changed to one of cold fury. "That is quite enough!"

"Sit down, Mr. Deene," Inspector Shah said firmly. "This is not helping matters."

"I'll sit down when I'm good and ready! She's my daughter! Do you hear me? She is *my* daughter! You and your selfish greed are going to get her killed!" He pointed an accusing finger at Lily's mother.

Lady Yarlbury looked stricken.

"Mr. Deene, we plan on doing everything we can to make sure she is returned unharmed," Shah said.

"He said, 'No police!' You heard him. I want you and your men out of here! Now!" David Deene shouted at Shah.

Lord Yarlbury stood. "*You* do not get to make that decision. You forfeited that right years ago when you abandoned your wife and child."

David Deene turned to stare at Lady Yarlbury. His mouth twisted into an ugly grimace. "Is that what you've told them?" he asked. "That I abandoned you? You didn't tell him that you were the one who left me. Why not, Maggie? Why didn't you tell him the truth? Why didn't you tell him that you took our daughter and left? You left me! You walked out on our marriage! Just like you are walking out on our daughter, right now!"

Inspector Shah caught the sergeant's eye and gave an almost imperceptible nod. The constable stepped in front of David Deene and grasped him firmly by the arm.

"Why don't we go outside for a bit of fresh air and cool down, sir?" the sergeant suggested, his tone friendly.

Deene yanked his arm free. He glared at everyone in the room. "If you insist on working with the police, her blood will be on your hands! Your hands!" he shouted before storming out of the flat. The door slammed shut behind him.

"He's afraid," Lily's mother said to no one in particular during the sudden silence that followed David Deene's exit. "He's angry because he's afraid."

So am I, thought Simon. *So am I.*

CHAPTER 20

THE BLITZ

1944
Spring

Heinrich couldn't believe it. He hadn't seen an orange since before the war. He lifted one out of the crate and held it up to his nose to breathe in the tangy citrus smell. It brought back memories of Christmas from when he was a little boy. His mother would hang a stocking at the end of his bed, and Christmas morning he would awake to find it filled with the most wonderful assortment of sweets and presents. At the very bottom, stuffed into the toe of his stocking, there was always a beautiful ripe orange.

"Careful, 'Arry," Jack warned. "Worth their weight in gold, those are. They keep careful count in the kitchen. Don't let one of 'em slip in your pocket." He slapped Heinrich good-naturedly on the back.

Heinrich carefully replaced the orange in the crate. As he lifted it, loud air raid sirens began to wail throughout the city. Startled, he almost dropped the crate.

"Bloody 'ell! The Jerries are back!" Jack shouted over the noise of the sirens. "Let's get this lot unloaded and get to the underground."

Jack climbed into the back of the lorry practically throwing the crates and bags of food at Heinrich as he raced to dump them in the empty kitchen. They worked quickly and silently; their only goal was to empty the truck, and as Jack so elegantly put it, "Get the 'ell out!" Heinrich tossed a sack of potatoes into the doorway. It ripped open, causing the potatoes to spill out and roll across the floor like large lumpy marbles. He didn't stop to pick them up. He didn't even break stride, just raced back to the lorry to grab another sack. Sweating and breathing hard, despite the cold night air, Jack and Heinrich emptied the lorry.

When the last crate was dropped in the kitchen. Jack locked the doors.

"This way," he shouted and took off limping quickly toward the street.

Heinrich followed him. This was the fourth bombing attack in as many weeks. It was amazing how quickly the air raid evacuations had become a normal part of everyone's life. Like Harry and Jack, an assortment of Londoners from all walks of life streamed onto the dark streets, most wearing heavy coats over pajamas, some of them carrying blankets or pillows, others with small picnic baskets. It wasn't unusual to see parents, many carrying small sleepy-eyed children hurrying to the underground metro as if they were heading off to start a family holiday instead of fleeing their homes. Everyone moved quickly, but surprisingly calmly, as they hastened toward their designated bomb shelters.

The siren's unrelenting wail paused momentarily, and Heinrich could hear the sound of the German warplanes grinding above them with an angry pulse, like bees buzzing in a cloud of blind fury. He looked up. The night sky was filled with dozens of tiny dazzling white lights as the planes released their incendiary bombs. They rained down from above like a strangely beautiful meteor shower illuminating the streets. As he watched, the white pinpricks of light seemed to go out one by one as they dropped to earth. Here and there, he could see a yellow flame leaped up from the white center as a bomb found its mark and a building or tree caught on fire somewhere in the distance.

He lost sight of Jack in the crowd but followed the others down the steps into the underground station. Finding a spot near the entrance where he could wait for the all-clear signal, he sat and listened to the muffled booms of the heavy bombs being dropped on London.

Four hours later, the "all clear" sounded. He stood, stiff from the damp and cold and, climbed up the steps to the street. Toward the east, the glow of distant fires tinted the early morning sky orange. The volunteer fire brigades would be out in force working to extinguish them. Only mildly worried, he started walking briskly toward the fires, toward Rachael's hospital.

The first thing he noticed was a small park, its leafless trees stripped bare of their bark from the blast of bombs. Broken glass crunched under his feet and the smell of burnt timber and brick dust filled the air. An anxious knot formed in the pit of his stomach as he walked past the damaged buildings. He quickened his pace. The destruction became more pronounced the closer he came to Rachel's hospital. Fear propelled him forward and he began running in the direction of her workplace. Dirt and brick dust filled his mouth and lungs as he ran through the rubble-filled streets.

When he finally reached the hospital, his heart lurched painfully in his chest at the scene before him. One side of the hospital building was crushed, as if smashed by a giant fist, the once stately iron gates reduced to a pile of bent and twisted metal. Dozens of tin-helmeted firefighters and medical personnel scurried about the area, shouting orders as they cleared bricks and timber, searching for survivors.

The injured sat or lay in the middle of the street, their faces dazed and bloodied. Heart hammering with fear, he frantically called her name, "Rachael!"

He moved among the injured searching for her, his gaze sweeping left and right as he walked, seeking out the white aprons of the nurses among the ambulance crews and ARP wardens. Where was she? "Please," he pleaded inwardly. "Please!"

Then he saw her, a small, slight figure bending over a man with a bloodied head. She had lost her nurse's cap and her dark hair had come loose, but she was unhurt. Relief flooded through him, leaving him weak in the knees. He closed his eyes and offered up a silent prayer of thanks.

His legs carried him to her. When he tapped her on the shoulder, she looked up expectantly. Before she could say anything, he gathered her into a crushing embrace and buried his face in her hair, breathing her in as if she were oxygen.

CHAPTER 21

AN UNDERGROUND SHELTER

December 8
5:30 p.m.

I ate the cheese sandwich slowly, washing down the dry white bread with another bottle of water. After I finished, I closed the lid.

"Harry?" I called out.

"I am here."

"I'm going to follow the wall all the way around the room and see if there is a vent or window or some way to get out of here."

"That is good."

I got back on my skinned knees and, pushing the cooler in front of me, once again crawled painfully across the brick floor. When the ice chest bumped up against a wall, I stopped.

The fact that I could hear Harry gave me hope that there was some sort of opening that I might be able to use to escape. I was determined to find it.

I stood up, pressing my back against the wall for support. Then, turning sideways, I ran my hands along the wall, which had a rough texture, cement, or maybe plaster. I wasn't sure. I could feel the defined edges of bricks in the places where cement had crumbled or worn away.

"I think the wall is made of brick like the floor," I said aloud. I ran my hand up as high as I could and was surprised to discover that my fingers brushed the wooden rafters of the ceiling.

"The ceiling is low. The room must be very small," I told him. I inspected the wall, patting the uneven surface with my hand from the floor to the ceiling. "No windows or vents here," I called out when I had finished.

I kept up a running commentary as I walked along the wall, describing what I found as I slowly, carefully circled the room. "Definitely brick." I rubbed my fingers feeling the mortar crumble as I did so. "Old. I think this is a very old building. The mortar is crumbling in some places."

I suspected that Harry knew all of this, but I found the sound of my own voice comforting. It filled the empty dark surrounding me as I made my slow circuit of the room.

My hand suddenly touched wood. "I've found the door!" I called out excitedly.

I felt a little bubble of hope rise up inside of me. Pressing both of my hands on the door, I pushed against it with all of my strength. It barely moved. Of course, it was locked. Most likely, bolted from the outside.

I continued to feel my way around the door and the frame. It was surprisingly small and narrow. There was nothing except two dime-sized holes in the place where a door handle should have been. I crouched down and pressed an eye against one of the holes. Not even the faintest light shone through.

I used my hands to explore. The wood was old, pitted, and worn. The metal hinges were rough and flaky with what I assumed must have been rust. A distant memory flickered in my mind. Something I saw once in a movie or read in a book about someone escaping by removing the hinges of a door. I felt a spark of something bright light up inside of me.

"Harry," I called out excitedly. "The door opens inward. If I can get the hinges off, maybe we can get out of here."

"You will need a tool."

"Yes," I agreed excitedly. "Maybe there is something in here. Something I can use."

I was energized now. A tool. I needed to find something hard that I could use to hammer the hinges loose.

I kept following the wall, moving slowly with short, shuffling steps, one hand on the wall beside me. When I reached the corner of the room, I paused, belatedly realizing that I should have counted my steps as a way to orient myself. I tried to remember how many I had taken. Not many. Maybe twelve or fifteen. *No matter,* I told myself. If I followed the wall, I knew I would find the door again.

I made the turn and continued on my way. After another half a dozen steps, my knee bumped into something.

I stretched out my hand.

"I found something," I told Harry.

Once again, using my hands to "see" for me, I explored the wood plank. It was smooth with legs like a shelf or a bench. If it was a shelf, perhaps someone had stored tools here. I slid my hands along the wood, hoping to find something I could use on the door hinges.

"It's a shelf, but there isn't anything on it," I said aloud.

I patted the wall from the bench to ceiling. It was solid. "No windows," I reported. "I'm going to keep going."

I stepped away from the wall so I could continue walking, one hand trailing the wall, my thigh brushing the wooden shelf as I moved. I was walking more quickly now, gaining confidence now that I had some sense of my surroundings.

"If there is a shelf, then maybe we'll get lucky. Someone must be using this place to store things," I told Harry. I had taken just a few steps when my bare foot came into contact with something hard and sharp. "Ow!" I yelped.

"You are hurt?" Harry asked, concerned.

"I'm fine," I told him. "I stepped on something."

My foot throbbing, I cautiously crouched down, patting the floor as I tried to find the thing I had stepped on. It was a broken brick. Feeling around with my hands, I discovered that the floor by this part of the wall was strewn with rubble, broken bricks, splintered boards, and dirt.

"Harry, there's a bunch of trash in here. Maybe I can find something I can use on the hinges," I called out excitedly.

I took a few careful steps over the debris and once again placed my hand on the wall. The bricks in this part were loose and crumbly, jutting out at crazy angles. Maybe I could break through to the other side! This could be my way out of here!

I began pushing and pulling on the loose bricks. "Harry," I called out excitedly. "I think I found a way out!"

I clawed with my fingers at the loose bricks, trying to pry them out of the wall. They didn't budge. I felt around on the floor until I found another broken brick. I picked it up and used it to hammer at the wall in front of me.

I beat on it until I was out of breath, then I ran my hands over the wall.

As I did so, I heard an ominous rumbling sound above my head. I froze and a cascade of dirt and rock showered down from above, filling my eyes and nose with grit and dust.

Coughing and wheezing, I called out to Harry. "Harry?

Are you okay?"

"This is not safe! You must go back!"

I had a sudden vision of the ceiling collapsing and being buried alive. There was another rumble and the beams above me creaked ominously. A jolt of fear washed through me. I backed up until the back of my legs came into contact with the wooden bench. Shaking, I sat down pressing my back against the solid brick wall behind me.

"Harry?" I called tentatively.

"I am here."

"I think we're underground."

"*Ja*."

"We are?"

"Yes."

"Are we in a cellar?"

"A shelter."

"A shelter? You mean like from a storm. Are we in a storm cellar?"

"No. It is a shelter from the bombs."

"Bombs?"

"*Ja*. The bombs. It is a shelter for the war. The airplanes drop the bombs and the people go in the shelter."

"You mean we're in an underground bomb shelter?"

"Yes."

I was suddenly struck by a new terrifying fear. I was in an underground room without any ventilation. Maybe I didn't need to worry about the walls caving in on me, maybe I needed to worry about suffocating. I could feel my heart rate quicken at the thought and I gulped as I tried to slow my breathing.

"Harry?"

"Ja?"

"How much air do you think is in here?" I asked in a small voice.

He was silent for a moment. "I do not know."

I inhaled, testing the air. Was I using up all the oxygen

in the room? How did you know when you were running out of air?

I pulled my wool blanket tightly around me, suddenly very conscious of each breath.

CHAPTER 22

A CHANCE ENCOUNTER

December 9
10:30 a.m.

The day was cold and gray. A few skeletal trees, their bare branches spindling skyward added to the atmosphere of bleak emptiness. To Simon everything around him seemed tinged with gray, as if all color and light had been drained from the city. Two days had passed,, and they were still no closer to finding Lily. His belly cramped with a hot, sour feeling at the thought.

He walked down the steps to the Tube station. Rush hour was long over so the crowd was sparse, which was probably why he noticed him. David Deene stood at the far end of the opposite train platform speaking with a man in a dark suit.

The man in the suit caught Simon's attention because he looked like he would have been more comfortable in a boxing ring than wearing a suit and tie. Big and burly with a shaved head, the man physically dominated David Deene.

Simon stared at the two men. He was too far away to hear their conversation, but it was obvious that the bald man was unhappy about something. He gestured abruptly and aggressively, punctuating his words by flinging his arm wide in either anger or frustration. *Not a pleasant man*, thought Simon. Though, the same could also be said of David Deene.

An arriving train blocked his view for a few moments and by the time the train departed, David Deene and the bald man were both gone.

Simon's train arrived a few minutes later and he boarded it, still thinking about the conversation he had witnessed. Whatever David Deene and the bald bloke had been arguing about, things hadn't gone Deene's way. That much was obvious from the body language.

Simon wondered who Lily's father would be meeting in London. Somebody from his work? A business deal gone bad, perhaps? He realized that he didn't know why her father had come to London; Simon doubted David Deene had come to England just to visit his daughter. Lily would have said something if she had known her father was in town. So why was David Deene in London? Business? Vacation? Perhaps it was time to find out.

Simon shook his head. It really didn't matter why her father was here. What mattered was Lily. His belly cramped with a hot, sour feeling again. The thought of her being held captive made him physically sick. He gripped the metal pole inside the train to steady himself and swallowed hard. He had to focus. Focus on staying calm and bringing her back to the people who loved her.

When he arrived at Lord Yarlbury's flat, Lily's mother let him in. Will was sitting on a small blanket in the middle of the living room floor happily chewing on a plastic toy of some sort. Lady Yarlbury noticed Simon glance at the baby and smiled fleetingly at him.

"Richard didn't want me to bring Will. He thought he should stay at Brynmoor with the nanny, but I couldn't leave him. I need the distraction. I don't think I could cope if I didn't have him here. He gives me something to do. It helps me take my mind off of … Lily." Her mouth trembled as she said Lily's name, and she looked away, her eyes brimming with tears.

Lady Yarlbury's sadness was hard to witness. Simon leaned toward her, wanting to help ease her pain but unsure of what to do. He felt undone both by Lily's absence and her mother's pain.

"So," she said, clearing her throat delicately as she worked to regain her composure. "Did Richard ask you to come and keep me company today?"

"I think we can both use the company," he said.

Will made a gurgling, giggling sound and they turned in unison to look at him.

"Yes," she replied without taking her eyes off Will. "It's hard to wait, isn't it? I think it's worse when you're alone. You can't distract yourself. Knowing that there is nothing I can do to bring her back … that the only thing I can do is wait is almost unbearable. I imagine you feel the same."

Simon felt his heart squeeze tight. It grew to an aching sadness that spread throughout his entire body. "Yes," he answered gruffly. "I do."

She sighed heavily and glanced over at Simon. "I don't know if Lord Yarlbury told you, but the police called. They found the car that was used to …" She paused and closed her eyes for a moment. "The car that they used to take Lily away. Apparently, they entered the parking garage. Somehow they had the code. The security cameras caught them."

A flicker of hope bumped under Simon's ribcage. Finding the car was progress. It means they were that much closer to finding Lily. "Do they know who they are? Have they identified them?"

Lady Yarlbury shook her head. "They were wearing

hats pulled low over their faces. The car was reported stolen earlier, but they have the forensics people looking at it. Maybe we'll get lucky. Richard is with the inspector now going over things. I'm supposed to wait here in case they call the flat instead of Richard's phone." She turned once again to watch Will playing. "They haven't called back since Richard told them that we want proof that she is unharmed. Richard and Inspector Shah told me that it doesn't mean anything, but I can't help but worry that … maybe she's hurt and she can't talk to us."

"They'll call," he told her. "We are going to get her back."

"We have to believe that, don't we?"

"Yes," he said fiercely. "Yes, we do."

The phone in the flat rang and both Lady Yarlbury and Simon started at the sound. Hand trembling, her ladyship picked up the receiver. She listened then sighed heavily.

"Thank you, Osmin. You may send him up," she said before replacing the old-fashioned receiver. "David's on his way up," she told Simon.

They waited without speaking until David Deene arrived. The doorbell rang and Lady Yarlbury opened it. Simon stood next to her, a silent pillar of support.

"Maggie," David Deene began speaking as soon as he entered the flat, ignoring Simon completely. "You've got to talk to Richard. You have to get him to tell the police to back off." He looked disheveled, nervous. His eyes were red-rimmed and haunted-looking. The belligerence and self-confidence he had exhibited earlier were gone.

So, Simon thought to himself, *Deene had been on the receiving end of the argument he had witnessed.*

Lady Yarlbury wrinkled her forehead. "David, I know you're worried."

"Dammit, Maggie!" Deene's fists were clenched, his voice shook with emotion. "You have to listen to me!"

His loud angry voice startled Will. He began to cry. Lady Yarlbury hurried over to him and picked him up, rocking and comforting him as David Deene looked on.

Desperate. The word popped into Simon's head. For the first time, he saw a man who was desperately afraid for his daughter.

Deene changed tactics and softened his tone, almost pleading with Lily's mother. "Maggie, you need to listen to me. We have to keep the police out of this. It's the only way to keep Lily safe. Richard needs to pay the money. If he does that, she'll be fine. She'll be safe as long as Richard pays."

He sounded like a man trying to convince himself that what he said was true, Simon thought.

Lady Yarlbury glanced at Simon. She reached out and touched David Deene's sleeve. "David, please believe me. We are doing everything we can to get her back safely. The police found the car that was used to take her. They are doing everything they can to help us find her."

"No, you don't understand!" Deene's voice rose again. "You have to get rid of that police inspector. No police! It's the only way to keep her safe!"

Lady Yarlbury's mobile rang. She looked at it where it was lying on top of the sofa table. She froze. "It's Lily's number," she whispered.

"Answer it," Deene snapped.

Cradling Will on her hip with one arm, she held the phone to her ear. "Hello?" she said shakily.

Simon's heart stilled.

"Yes," she said, the word barely a whisper.

As she listened, the blood drained from her face and her hand began to shake uncontrollably. She swayed on her feet. Simon reached out an arm to steady her. The phone dropped from her grasp.

She looked up at him, her face deathly pale. "He said if we didn't stop talking to the police, he would kill her."

"I'll call Lord Yarlbury," Simon told her as he gently led her to the sofa.

"Tell him we have the proof he's asked for," Deene

said. He thrust his hand in his coat pocket and drew out a small manila envelope, dumping the contents over the sofa table. "This arrived at my hotel this morning."

A small silver bracelet spilled onto the glass top.

Lady Yarlbury and Simon stared at the bracelet.

"Here's your proof!" Deene snapped angrily. "Richard wanted proof. Well, here it is! I gave this to Lily the day before they took her." He collapsed in one of the armchairs and buried his head in his hands.

CHAPTER 23

A NOTE UNDER THE DOOR

1944
Mid-spring

Love had made them careless. He could see that now. The sheer wonder of it all, the thrill of finding such unexpected happiness had caused them to behave foolishly and someone had noticed. Heinrich reread the anonymous note they had found thrust under the door. It was ugly and threatening. The note contained one word, written in capital letters: *TRAITOR*.

Rachael looked up at him, her eyes wide and frightened. "What does it mean? Why would someone write this?"

It was his fault. He should have left after that first night. Because he stayed, he had put Rachel at risk. *TRAITOR*. He was the traitor. He had deserted his unit and his country, but if he was caught, Rachel would be the one who paid the price.

"Someone knows of me. They know who I am," he said with a sick hollow feeling in the pit of his stomach.

She shook her head vehemently. "No! That's not possible! How could they know?"

Heinrich held the small square of paper out to her. "Someone knows."

She snatched the paper from his hand and crumpled it into a tight wad. "No, they don't. They don't know anything," she insisted. "No one knows anything. It's someone's idea of a sick joke. They don't know about you!"

"I have to leave."

"No!" Rachael said fiercely.

"Rachel," he said sadly. "There is no other way. They know who I am."

Rachel's looked at him, her expression mulish, her eyes shining with a fierce light. "No, they don't! They don't know about you. How could they? No one knows who you are! They think you're my cousin! No one knows!"

"Rachel—" he began.

She held up her hand, stopping him from continuing. "No! They don't really know. Mr. Blackthorn, he asked me if you were foreign. He said he heard you talking. He wrote the note! I know he wrote it! I'll go talk to him. I can explain your accent. I can tell him you are Polish or Swiss. I'll tell him you emigrated here. There are lots of people who have emigrated. He would believe me." She spoke quickly, her words tumbling over one another.

"No," Heinrich told her gently. "I have to go."

"Maybe it was Mrs. Wallace," she continued as if he hadn't spoken. "It could have been Mrs. Wallace. She asked me about you. She wanted to know why you weren't going back to fight in the war. Maybe she wrote the note."

He reached out to her and took her hand. "Rachael, I have to go away. To protect you."

"No, no, no!" Rachael whispered, her eyes filling with tears. "You can't leave. Where will you go? If they find you, they will kill you. I can hide you. We can find a place for you to hide."

He gazed at her tenderly and shook his head. "No. I must go. I have no choice. If they find me here with you … if they know you are helping me … you cannot explain. I must do this."

Every part of him wanted to stay, to keep her close and protect her, but he knew the only way he could protect her was to leave. "I will go tonight."

She threw herself into his arms and hugged him fiercely as tears ran down her cheeks.

"When the war is over," he whispered. "We will be together. When the war is over."

She argued with him to stay a few more nights so that she could find some place safe where he could hide. She spoke urgently, her eyes filled with fevered light. "I can call my uncle. He has a farm in Yorkshire. You can stay with him. I'll tell him you are a refugee from Germany. You will be safe there. No one will question the fact that he has hired a foreign laborer. All I need to do is find someone to cover my shift tomorrow. Maybe Sheila. She might do it. I'll call my uncle. I'll tell the hospital that I had a family emergency. I'll ask Sheila tonight after I call my uncle and then we can leave for Yorkshire tomorrow."

He allowed her to believe that she had convinced him. He didn't want to spend their last evening together arguing. He nodded.

She sighed with relief. "I'll call him now. You're going to like him. I know you will."

After she made the phone calls, they ate their last dinner together. He had no appetite for food, but he managed to swallow the meal and even to feign interest as she described her uncle's family and farm. He would do anything, make any sacrifice necessary to keep her safe, which was why he had to leave. Tonight.

CHAPTER 24

AN AMERICAN CITIZEN

December 9
Noon

David Deene had plausible explanation. The manila envelope with the necklace had mysteriously appeared in his hotel room. Simon didn't believe him, but there would be no police investigation to verify Deene's story.

After the call to Lady Yarlbury's mobile, Simon rang his lordship. Lord Yarlbury returned to the flat with Inspector Shah within the hour. There was an ugly row with David Deene. This time, however, Lady Yarlbury had joined forces with her ex-husband and pressured his lordship to send the inspector away. Reluctantly, Inspector Shah acquiesced.

Now there would be no one to interview the hotel staff or review video from the security cameras. No one to identify who delivered the bracelet to David Deene's hotel room, *if* someone delivered the bracelet to his hotel room.

Simon couldn't help but think that the lack of investigation was convenient for Lily's father. Simon's thoughts returned to the meeting he had witnessed between David Deene and the bald man. The meeting that occurred less than an hour before he arrived at the flat with the silver bracelet.

There was something off about David Deene. Something off about the whole situation. Jenna's words echoed in his head: *"What are you doing to find Lily?"*

Simon decided that it was time for him to do something. When Lily's father exited the flat, Simon followed him. He trailed him several blocks to the Tube station, keeping well back.

David Deene looked up as Simon boarded the same train, catching Simon's gaze. He frowned slightly. Simon nodded politely. Hoping that Lily's father assumed their being on the same train was a coincidence. He might have gotten away with it, but Deene changed trains and Simon was forced to do the same.

It was impossible to hide on the train, especially if you happened to be six-three and ginger-haired, though Simon did his best to be discreet. This time, he chose a different train carriage from that of Lily's father. He stood by doors and watched the passengers as they disembarked from the other carriage, hoping that he wouldn't lose sight of David Deene in the crush of passengers getting on and off the trains.

He almost did. David Deene waited until the last moment to disembark, exiting in a crowd of people. Fortunately, Simon was able to use his size and quick reflexes to push his way out just as the doors of his carriage were closing.

Deene exited the underground at Vauxhall and headed toward the Riverwalk. Simon followed. Lily's father walked briskly, Simon trailing behind him along the south bank of the River Thames. After a few minutes, the distinctive building of the American Embassy appeared in front of them, sitting like a giant sugar cube in the middle of a puddle tea.

Was Deene going to the embassy or staying at one of the hotels nearby? Simon wondered, hoping it was the latter.

It wasn't. David Deene showed his passport to the embassy guards and entered the building. Simon watched and waited. Why was Deene at the embassy? Was he reporting Lily's disappearance to the Americans? Seeking their help?

Simon took up a post near the front, where he could keep an eye on the entrance. He'd been there about thirty minutes when he noticed two British police officers detach themselves from the front entrance and saunter along the walk in his direction.

He was completely taken by surprise when they stopped directly in front of him.

"Sir, you'll need to leave the area." The officer's words were polite but firm.

"Me?" Simon asked, surprised, his gaze shifting between the two police officers.

"Yes."

"Why? Has something happened?" he asked worriedly.

The two officers exchanged glances. "Sir, you've been asked to leave the area. Are you refusing to leave?"

"No. Of course not."

"Then I suggest you move along."

Simon glanced at the front entrance of the American Embassy as he walked back the way he'd come. He had no doubt that this was David Deene's doing, but there was nothing he could do about it. Though it did beg the question, why was Deene so keen on keeping Simon away? What was he hiding?

CHAPTER 25

A NEW PLAN

December 9
Noon

My attempt to dislodge the hinges of the door hadn't worked. I hadn't found any tools in my cautious search of the rubble. I tried to pry them loose using a nail as a wedge and a brick as a hammer. Despite my efforts, the hinges were still attached to the door and all I'd managed to do was smash my thumb badly. So, I created a new plan. Harry didn't like it, but I had run out of alternatives.

My new plan was simple. Make a weapon. Attack the man with the mask.

Escape.

I cautiously made my way back to the rubble and searched until I found what I needed. When I returned, I drank the last bottle of water, placed the empty bottle in the cooler, and shoved the cooler toward the middle of the room.

Then I sat by the door, cloaked in darkness, and waited for the masked man to return, one hand clutching a brick, the other hand holding a shard of broken glass.

CHAPTER 26

THE ROOT CELLAR

1944
Hours Later

The air raid sirens sounded just as they finished washing up the dishes. Heinrich and Rachel looked at each other without speaking. Heinrich folded the dish towel. Rachel put the last of the dishes in the cupboard. He walked to the hall closet and took out her coat, holding it for her. Her mouth trembled as she slipped her arms into the sleeves.

"Oh, Harry," she said. "I wanted tonight to be special."

He grinned crookedly at her before folding her into a gentle hug. "It is special. I am with you," he said. They stood there not speaking, enjoying each other for a moment. Then, sighing heavily, Heinrich stepped out of the embrace. "Come. We must go."

She wiped her eyes, nodding.

Heinrich put on his coat and took two heavy blankets

down from the closet shelf. They left the flat, carefully locking the door behind them, and joined the other residents as they quietly filed down the stairwell and out into the back garden.

The night air was cold and damp. Wraiths of fog curled around the buildings and shrubs, giving the garden an eerie ghostly appearance. No one spoke as the residents queued patiently waiting for Mr. Blackthorn to check them off his list.

This British quiet stoicism was something that Heinrich greatly admired. He knew that even as the London streets filled with people making their way to the public bomb shelters, there would be no pushing or shoving, but rather calm progression of families and individuals nodding to friends and helping neighbors. It was all very orderly and civilized despite the ominous wailing of sirens.

The elderly Mr. Blackthorn, their local air raid warden, stood in the back garden, looking resplendent in his blue uniform and steel helmet, a white lanyard across his chest. He held a clipboard in front of him, checking off the names of the residents as they filed past.

The residents of each flat had been assigned to one of the two shelters. A government-issued Anderson shelter in the back garden, its corrugated metal roof just visible under a mound of dirt freshly planted with Mr. Wallace's turnips and cabbages, and an old root cellar that had been part of the original Victorian manor house.

Heinrich and Rachel queued behind Mrs. Hopley, her married daughter, and her two young grandchildren. Rachel linked her arm through his and nodded politely to them. The two women stared curiously at Heinrich but were too polite to say anything.

"Rachel Cohen," Mr. Blackthorn announced, placing a check next to her name. "Very good." He handed her a gas mask.

"Thank you." Rachel smiled winningly at him. "You remember my cousin Harry," she said. "Have you added him to your list?"

He gave Harry a stern look. "I don't have a mask for him. He's not on the official list."

"That's all right. The masks make Harry nervous." She lowered her voice conspiratorially. "Bad memories from the war, you know how it is."

"Ahh, well." Mr. Blackthorn cleared his throat. "Exactly how much longer will your cousin be staying with you?" he asked her.

Rachel shook her head sadly. "The doctors say that it could be months and months before his nerves are better. Shell shock is a tricky thing, but with your war experience, I suspect you already know that."

Mr. Blackthorn glanced at Heinrich, who gazed blankly over the old man's shoulder, trying to look suitably shell shocked. Mr. Blackthorn cleared his throat again. "Well, yes. I do hope he is making progress on that front. Last name?" he asked Heinrich.

"Cohen," Rachel answered quickly before he could reply.

Mr. Blackthorn wrote Harry Cohen next to Rachel's name on the list. "The two of you will be in the root cellar."

Rachel smiled gratefully at Mr. Blackthorn as she tugged on Heinrich's arm. "Come along, Harry. Don't fret about the sirens. They'll stop soon enough."

During Victorian times, the underground root cellar had been used to store vegetables and other items for use in the manor house kitchen until the invention of electricity and refrigeration made the cellar obsolete. For years the root cellar had languished as a place to toss rusty tools and leftover paint cans, but the war had changed that. Because of the German air raids, the cellar was once again in use, this time as a bomb shelter.

The only entrance to the cellar was a small rectangular opening cut into the ground along the back side of the house. A set of narrow stairs led down to a door that opened directly into the small room.

As they descended the steps to the root cellar, Heinrich had to stoop to avoid hitting his head on the door lintel. He made a mental note to remind Rachel to request the Anderson shelter from now on. It wasn't as comfortable as the 150-year-old root cellar, but the Anderson shelters offered better protection; their iron beams provided structural support while the corrugated tin roofs flexed and absorbed the concussive impact of the German explosives. On his travels across London, he had seen the tin roofs of the Anderson shelters poking up through the rubble of bombed-out buildings, like flower blooms springing up from freshly tilled earth. He didn't think that the old bricks and crumbling mortar of the cellar would provide the same level of protection if a bomb were to explode nearby.

Mr. Blackthorn and the residents had done what they could to make the cellar as comfortable as possible, but as a temporary home for four adults and two children, it still was rather cramped and cold. A wooden bench had been fixed to one wall and two army cots had been assembled for the children. A lantern hung on a peg from the ceiling.

The Hopley grandchildren happily sprawled across one of the cots. The girl brought a set of pastels and paper with her, the boy an erector set. The mother gave Rachel a quick, harried smile as she made up the second cot with blankets and pillows. Old Mrs. Hopley sat on a pillow she had placed upon the hard, wooden bench. She pulled her knitting out of a bag, nodding politely to Rachel. "Good evening, my dear."

Heinrich laid one of the blankets atop the bench. He and Rachel sat on it, then pulled the second blanket over them. He leaned back against the rough brick wall. Rachel laid her head on his shoulder as they waited for the German bombers, hoping they wouldn't drop their bombs on their little garden tonight.

CHAPTER 27

WAITING

December 10
9:00 p.m.

He should have expected it, he realized. He told Jenna not to come to London, but he should have known better. She had never listened to him in the past and certainly wasn't going to start now, as she loudly explained to him when he opened the door.

Jenna, alone, he might have been able to handle. Unfortunately, she had brought reinforcements, their cousin Ben. The two of them sat on Paul's sofa, grilling him for information. Jenna, unhappy that no one was telling her anything about her missing best friend, kept insisting that he was withholding information from her.

She was right, but that didn't change the fact that he wasn't about to tell them anything that might jeopardize Lily's life. He needed both Jenna and Ben to leave. There was too much at stake.

"Go home," he told Jenna after going several rounds with her. "There is nothing you can do here.

"You need to tell us what's going on," his sister demanded, her blue eyes sparking dangerously.

Simon held his sister's gaze, fighting to tamp down the impatience and frustration. "I've told you all I can."

She narrowed her eyes at him. "All you can, or all you know?" she asked.

Ouch! Sometimes his sister was too smart for her own good. "Look, Jenna, the police are doing everything they can to find her. That is what I can tell you, and that is what I know. The police are interviewing people. They are talking to everyone and anyone who might know anything. They are doing their job. They are taking care of things. There is nothing you can do here to help. You're not going to be able to do anything the police are doing right now."

"All right, the police are interviewing people. We get that. They are doing their job. We get that too. So, what are *you* doing here?" Ben challenged. "If you're so confident that the police are taking care of things, why are you still in London?"

Simon exhaled slowly, working to keep his temper in check. He was beyond exhausted and stressed. He didn't want to have a row with Jenna and Ben. He knew they were worried. Everyone who loved Lily was worried and frustrated and afraid. The problem was that he needed them to leave. Things were going to start happening. He didn't have time to deal with the two of them, and he didn't want them to muck things up.

Simon looked directly at Ben. "I am in London because I am helping Lord Yarlbury."

"Helping Lord Yarlbury? How?"

Simon gritted his teeth. "I've been at the university talking to people, showing her photo, asking if anyone saw her."

"I thought you said the police were doing that?" Jenna countered.

"They are, but … well, I have to do something."

Jenna nodded. "Right. So, what have you found out?"

He shook his head. "I can tell you that Lord Yarlbury said that the police have a very promising lead and they are following it."

"What kind of lead?" Jenna asked suspiciously.

Simon held up his hand before Ben could interject. "They found the car that was used to kidnap Lily."

Jenna turned to Ben. "They found the car. That has to be good, right?"

"It's something, I guess," he conceded. "Look, I promise to ring you the minute I hear anything, but right now I'm knackered. I want to go to bed, and you two happen to be sitting on my bed."

It took a bit more convincing, but Jenna and Ben finally agreed to leave.

"Fine. You ring me the minute you hear anything," Jenna insisted.

"I will," he promised.

After Jenna and Ben left, Simon stretched out on the sofa, emotionally and physically spent.

He was in a dark tunnel. He could hear Lily crying. She was hurt! He couldn't see her. He called out to her.

Lily was calling for him! She needed help!

"I'm coming!" Blindly, he began to run. Shouting her name, he stumbled through the dark, searching for her.

She answered, but he couldn't understand. What was she was saying? Her voice was faint, as if she were answering from far away. He needed to find her!

He began to run faster. He couldn't find her! "Lily!" he called. She didn't answer. She was leaving him!

"Lily! Where are you?" he shouted. "Don't leave. Come back to me!"

There was no answer.

Simon jolted out of his dream in a cold sweat, his heart

hammering against his ribs. It took him a moment to remember where he was. He lay in the dark, the details of his dream replaying over and over in his head, his stomach churning with anxiety. He sat up, exhaling slowly through his nose, compressing his fear and anxiety into a tight ball with the force of his diaphragm. He needed to stay calm and focused. Fear was a distraction he could not afford.

Grabbing his mobile, he checked the time. One a.m. He leaned back against the sofa, gripping his mobile tightly. There was nothing to do now but wait for Lord Yarlbury to call him once we received the ransom drop site. He prayed they were doing the right thing.

Inspector Shah's ominous words from their last meeting still pricked at Simon. "I don't recommend going at it alone," he had warned them before leaving. "Kidnappings do not always end well. It's often easier to get rid of the evidence than it is to take the risk of delivering a body."

"She'll be fine. All we need to do is pay them and keep the police away," Deene had spoken with a self-assurance none of them felt after the door closed behind the inspector. "She'll be fine. We just need to do what he says, and she'll be fine."

The anonymous caller must have been watching the flat, because shortly after the inspector left, Lily's mother had received a second phone call.

"Wait for my call," the voice had rasped. "Remember. No police or she dies."

Now there was nothing to do but wait.

CHAPTER 28

DRIFTING IN THE DARK

December 11
Midnight

The darkness made time slip away into a dreamless mist. Day or night, life or death, it was all the same. All I knew was despair, so profound that I did not even think of it as despair. The person I knew as me had ceased to exist. I floated in a black void.

I was no longer shivering. I no longer felt the cold. In fact, I no longer felt much of anything. I was tired, very tired. My limbs were heavy, as if they were made of lead. I closed my eyes. Darkness wrapped itself around me like a blanket, and my body slid to the ground like a stone sinking into deep, murky water.

We were riding the horses in Sheldon Wood. Simon led us onto the narrow bridle path. I followed behind. He rode with an easy athletic grace and I admired his straight strong back and his broad shoulders. Sunlight filtered through the leafy canopy overhead, and I sighed, happy to enjoy the beauty of the lush green wood and Simon's company. Simon turned to look at me, his expression troubled and anxious. It was then that I noticed I was floating. I drifted skyward, moving farther and farther away as Simon stared up at me.

"Come back to me," he called out, but I just kept floating farther away.

Suddenly, as if someone had abruptly changed the channel, Simon disappeared.

"Open your eyes!" A voice shouted at me. "You must open your eyes!"

"Leave me alone," I mumbled.

"You must open your eyes!" he shouted again. "You must not sleep!"

I tried to ignore the shouting, but the voice was relentless, and it was making my head hurt. He shouted angrily at me. "Open your eyes!"

I was so tired. All I wanted to do was sleep.

"You must not sleep! OPEN YOUR EYES!"

Each word was like a nail being hammered into the back of my skull. I managed to pry my eyes open. I just wanted him to stop shouting. I thought if I opened my eyes, he would leave me alone.

"I'm tired," I complained, slurring my words.

"If you sleep now you will not wake up again! OPEN YOUR EYES!"

His words slowly penetrated the fog in my brain.

"SIT UP!"

I dragged myself into a sitting position. "Why are you shouting at me?" I asked my head pounding with the effort. I rubbed my eyes, my arms and hands clumsy with fatigue.

"You are too cold," Harry said. I could hear the relief in his voice. "You must not sleep. Also, the air is bad, I think."

He was wrong. I didn't feel cold, I just felt tired.

"I will talk, and you will listen, but *you must not sleep*!"

I nodded. "Okay."

"I will tell you about Rachel."

Rachael? I asked groggily.

"My beautiful angel," he said.

I rested my pounding head on my knees and closed my eyes as I listened to Harry talk about his Rachel, for that was how he referred to her, "My Rachel." It was sweet. He had saved her, and she had taken him in. As he talked, I found myself growing increasingly sleepy again.

My headache turned into a dull throb. I was exhausted, so exhausted.

There was something I was supposed to do, but I couldn't quite remember what it was. I tried to catch hold of the thoughts swirling about in my brain, but they drifted away, disappearing into the air like wisps of smoke. I lay down, the chore of inhaling and exhaling becoming increasingly difficult.

Harry was talking to me, but now his voice seemed to come from farther away—it became weaker and weaker, until it turned into a faint, buzzing noise. Now Simon was talking to me. Why didn't they leave me alone?

I closed my eyes and let myself drift away. Weightless and senseless, I drifted on a gentle black sea. Feeling nothing. Wanting nothing but to sleep.

From somewhere far away, I heard barely audible voices echoing strangely, as if I was listening to them in a tunnel.

"Bloody hell, she don't look so good."

Someone nudged me. I tried to open my eyes, but they were too heavy. I felt a warm hand on my neck, checking my pulse.

"Is she dead?" a second voice asked.

"No."

"Then pull her out of there and get her some air."

Someone grabbed me under the arms and dragged me through the door. I felt warm, stale breath wash over me and the hand on my neck again. "She looks done in."

"As long as she isn't dead."

"She's got a pulse."

"Right then. Tie her up and put her in the boot."

I inhaled and felt the buzzing in my head again. I didn't want to go in the boot. I wanted to tell them, but I couldn't seem to get my mouth to work properly.

"I don't think that's such a good idea. She looks bad. Maybe she needs air."

"Put in her in the boot. We need to move her."

"I can blindfold her and tie her up, then we can put her in the back."

"No. We're too close to the nick. What if one of them cozzers gets it in their heads to stop and have a look in the back? What happens then? You do what I tell you to do. Put her in the boot."

"I don't think we should put her in the boot," the second voice insisted stubbornly.

"Do what I tell you."

"You do it then. I don't want to be mixed up in any killing."

"Bloody hell!" the first voice snapped. I was vaguely aware of being lifted before once again letting myself drift away.

CHAPTER 29

THE DROP

December 11
2:00 a.m.

Simon's mobile rang. "Hullo?"

"They called," Lord Yarlbury said, his voice grim. "Hampstead Heath. I'm to leave the money under the bench at Saint Boudicca's Barrow. When they have the money, they will call and tell me where Lily is."

"I'm off then."

"You'll need to take care, Simon."

"They won't see me," Simon assured him. "I'll find a place to leave the car and walk up from Millfield Lane. It isn't safe for you to go alone, and if Lily needs medical attention, I'll be able to give it to her."

There was a brief pause on the line before Lord Yarlbury's calm, leveled voice replied, "Right then. Take care."

"You too, Your Lordship."

At first, his lordship hadn't been keen on Simon accompanying him, but he eventually agreed that carrying a large sum of money to a dark, isolated location without protection was dangerous. The two of them hatched a plan. His lordship would deliver the money alone as demanded. Simon would follow, providing protection for Lord Yarlbury and, if possible, trail the person who received the money, improving their chances of finding Lily. They had told neither Lily's mother nor David Deene of their plan.

Simon left Paul's flat, careful to close the door softly so as not to wake him. He hurried down the front steps to his car.

The predicted winter cold snap had finally arrived. An icy wind gusted along the darkened street, sending a stray piece of cellophane skittering along the sidewalk. He had chosen to wear his mackintosh because the dark color would make him less conspicuous in the night, but now given the turn in the weather, he was very glad of the choice. It had begun to rain, a frigid rain that held the promise of sleet or possible snow flurries. He pulled the collar of his mac tight as he walked along the street to his parked car.

An anxious energy hummed through his veins and his chest felt tight. He reached into his pocket and pulled out the car keys, noticing with an almost clinical detachment that his hands were shaking. Unlocking his car, he climbed inside. It took him two tries to insert the key. He paused, resting his hands on the steering wheel. Nerves were a distraction he couldn't afford. Not now. Not when there was so much at stake. Inhaling deeply, he held his breath for a count of three before exhaling slowly, slowing his heart rate, forcing himself to concentrate on the one and only thing that mattered. Lily. *Focus on the task*, he told himself. Nothing else mattered. Start the car. Drive to the Heath. Keep his lordship safe. Find Lily. Focus on the task. His hands steadied. He turned the key in the ignition.

It was time to bring Lily home.

Raindrops intermixed with small ice pellets bounced across the windscreen as the car sped along the dark, slick streets. Simon switched on the wipers allowing the rhythmic sound to soothe him as he drove. He was going to bring Lily home. He wouldn't allow, couldn't allow, any alternative to that belief. Lily was coming home. Lord Yarlbury would pay the ransom and they would bring Lily home.

When he arrived at the heath, he pulled onto High Gate West. He drove slowly, the wet asphalt gleaming under the streetlamps as he searched for an inconspicuous place to park. He found a likely spot, pulled over, and switched off the ignition. Next, he changed his mobile to silent, then simply sat in the dark, listening as the rain thrummed on the roof of his car. Five minutes later, Lord Yarlbury's Mercedes drove past. Simon waited a few moments to ensure that no other cars had followed his lordship before exiting his car.

Pulling the hood of his mac over his head, he began to walk along the shoulder of the road. He crossed over to Milford Lane, leaving the last of the streetlights behind him. A weak, watery moonlight spilled onto the crooked trunks and leafless limbs of the trees bordering the lane, giving them a sinister appearance. He thrust his hands in his pockets and hunched his shoulders against the cold half-frozen rain that pelted him from above.

He entered the heath, ducking onto the walking path that crossed over Highgate ponds, and began walking in the direction of Queen Boudicca's barrow. The heath was deserted. He could hear nothing but the steady tapping of the icy raindrops as they struck the surface of the ponds and the occasional rushing gust of wind.

Queen Boudicca's grave was located at the top of a hill surrounded by a copse of trees. It was a clever choice, Simon conceded. The person who had taken Lily had planned carefully. The location of the grave mound offered an unobstructed view of anyone climbing the hill. It would be almost impossible for anyone to stake out the gravesite without being seen.

In addition, the walking paths that wandered through this part of the heath wound their way among ancient woodlands, grassy vales, ponds, and playgrounds crossing and re-crossing themselves, making it difficult if not impossible to follow anyone. Any person wishing to make sure they were not being followed, could simply step off the path and conceal themselves from prying eyes among the trees and shrubbery.

Yes, for a clandestine meeting this was a good choice. Although, it also worked to Simon's advantage. The same trees that sheltered his prey could also provide cover for him. Simon stepped off the path, melting into the shadows, his shoulders hunched against the weather, his eyes searching for movement in the surrounding darkness.

From where he stood, Simon could see a small circle of light bobbing along the walking path. *Lord Yarlbury's torch*, he thought as he watched it climb steadily upward. The light suddenly stopped moving and appeared to wobble in midair. His lordship must have reached the barrow.

Simon watched as the light dipped momentarily, then moved in a sweeping arc, before winking out for a brief moment. He held his breath and listened intently. The light winked back on, bobbing up and down like a glowing ball floating on a black sea. *He's just placed the bag of money under the bench*, Simon thought. The small circle of light hovered in the air for a moment before it began to trace a path away from Queen Boudicca's grave.

Simon waited in the shrubbery, his gaze shifting between the light of Lord Yarlbury's torch and the dark shadows surrounding the barrow. As his lordship turned off the path into the trees, his body obscured the beam of his torch. It appeared that his lordship was safely away. Now they just had to wait and hope that the person who collected the money fulfilled their side of the bargain.

Eyes straining, Simon watched for movement on the heath. He thought he heard something. His body stilled. He rocked silently on the balls of his feet, his shoulders and neck tense. The wet branches creaked as a fierce blast of wind gusted through the shrubbery. Shivering, his eyes locked like lasers onto the barrow.

Simon heard the engine before he saw the headlamp. He followed its movement with his eyes as it traveled up the hill to the barrow. A motorbike. Bloody hell! There would be no chance of following him on foot now.

Shaking with frustration and anger, Simon watched as the motorbike paused at the top of the hill, the driver throttling back the engine as he searched for the money. It took him less than a minute. The engine's roar echoed in the night air as the motorbike cut through the copse at the top of the hill and raced off into the night. They had the money, and there was absolutely nothing he could do about it! There was nothing he could do at all except wait. Wait and hope and pray that they returned Lily.

Simon wrenched his mobile out of his pocket and rang Lord Yarlbury. "They have the money. He's on a motorbike. I've no way of following him."

"Right then," came the terse reply. "I'll drive round to your car. Where did you park?"

Simon described where he had left the car, ended the call, and took off running.

Breathless, he arrived at his car before Lord Yarlbury. Rather than unlock it and wait inside, he stood head down, hands thrust in his pockets, as the icy rain fell and sent up a silent plea. "Please," he begged. "Please let her be safe."

Lord Yarlbury's Mercedes rounded the bend, the sleet glinting silver in the car's headlights. Simon stepped out into the road and raised an arm. His lordship stopped the car and Simon climbed into the passenger side.

"Nothing yet," Lord Yarlbury said before Simon could ask.

They waited in tense silence for the call. A sort of

churning stillness settled over the two of them and Simon stared out the windscreen, watching the sleet and raindrops as they bounced off the hood of the car and onto the road. As each agonizing minute ticked passed, Simon's fear grew. His body felt strung as tight as a high wire. His stomach clenched with anxiety. Were they doing the right thing? He kept replaying the inspector's horrifying phrase inside his head, *"It's easier to get rid of the evidence."*

Resolutely, he pushed the words from his mind. They were going to bring Lily home. He focused on that one and only thought. Lily was coming home. There was no alternative.

When the call finally came, Simon felt as if he'd been kicked in the stomach. The call was short, two words: Brixton Market.

His lordship drove quickly, his expression grim. Adrenaline pricked under Simon's arms as they wound their way through the streets toward the market. He silently willed Lord Yarlbury to drive faster. His lordship turned onto Atlantic Road and slowed the Mercedes to a crawl. The street was empty. They rolled past Brady's clock tower, the market's battered and neglected landmark, as the icy rain began to fall in earnest. Half-frozen drops poured down upon them in sheets, creating pools of muddy water on the road in front of them. Visibility was incredibly poor. Simon leaned forward, straining to see. Where was she?

He thought he spotted something up ahead on the side of the road. He couldn't quite make out what it was, but something lay on the ground, illuminated by a halo of light cast from a nearby streetlamp. He narrowed his eyes.

"There she is!" His voice was louder than he had intended. He pointed, yanking open the passenger door and leaping out before Lord Yarlbury was able to stop the car. Heart hammering in his chest, he rushed across the street.

They had dumped her like so much rubbish on the sidewalk. She lay on her side, wearing only an oversize cotton shirt. Her eyes were closed. She lay still, lifeless.

He bent over her, reached out, and touched the side of her neck. Her skin was wet and deathly cold. For a terrible heart-wrenching moment, he thought she was dead, but then he felt it. Her pulse was weak and thready, but it was there!

Simon climbed into the back of his lordship's Mercedes, cradling her in his arms. "She's hypothermic. Her body temperature is dangerously low. She needs to go directly to the hospital."

Lord Yarlbury nodded, waited for Simon to close the door, then stepped on the gas.

As the Mercedes lurched forward, Simon shrugged out of his mac and lifted Lily's wet shirt over her head. He pulled her close, using his body heat to warm her. He had to raise her temperature slowly. Too quickly and she could go into shock, too slowly and her organs would continue to shut down. He wrapped his mac around her back and held her tightly against his chest, counting every impossibly slow beat of her heart. He buried his face in her wet hair. "You'll be all right, now. I've got you," he whispered.

CHAPTER 30

AWAKE

December 11

It was like slowly waking from a deep, deep sleep. I had the faintest awareness of a noise, like the lapping of waves against the shore. *Thump. Thump. Thump.* A strong, steady rhythm hovered on the far edges of my mind as I drifted. *Thump. Thump. Thump.* The strength and warmth of Simon's steady heartbeat spread through me, pulling me to the surface once again.

I was aware of blurring lights, colors, and echoes. Everything was a jumble of images and noise, none of which made any sense or formed any sort of coherent pattern in my mind. It was like looking at something through a kaleidoscope. I couldn't seem to put the pieces together to form a picture. Trying to do so left me feeling dizzy and weak, so I simply closed my eyes.

Eventually I woke up in a hospital bed with an IV in my arm and my mouth so dry that my tongue felt like it was glued to the top of my mouth. I lay in a room bathed in artificial light. I lay still for a long while, trying to figure out where I was. All I knew was that I was in a bed that wasn't my own, in a room that smelled of antiseptic. I was covered with a blanket, but I was still cold. I wondered if I could get another blanket. I turned my head and I saw that Simon was sitting in a chair next to my bed, asleep.

At first, I wasn't certain if I was really seeing him or if I was dreaming. I stared at him quietly, drinking him in. His strawberry blond hair was darker now, though it still carried some blond highlights left from a summer of chasing sheep and horses around Shropshire. He looked tired and drawn, as if he hadn't slept in a long time.

He stirred and glanced over at me. When he saw that I was awake, his eyes flew open, joy lighting up his face. "Lily! You're awake." He grinned from ear to ear as if he had just won the lotto.

I looked at him, confused. "Simon, where am I?"

"You're at the hospital. You've had a rough go of things," he told me, his smile dimming. "God! You gave me a proper scare. Are you feeling all right?"

"I don't understand." I tried to sit up, only I didn't seem to have any strength. My arms and legs felt heavy and cumbersome, as if they were made of cement or stone instead of flesh and blood.

"Take it easy," Simon said gently. "Let me help you."

He stood and raised the bed for me, adjusting the pillows behind my back.

"How is that then?"

I managed a wan smile. "Better." I held out my hand to him.

He brushed the back of my hand with his lips. "So am I. Now that you're on the mend," he said, his voice husky with emotion.

"Simon, how did I …? Where …? What …? I don't remember …" I seemed to be having a hard time forming complete thoughts.

"Shhh. It's best you rest for a bit and get your strength back."

"But ..."

"Shhh. Just rest for a bit. I've got to call your mum."

"My mom?"

"She'll want to know you're awake. I promised I'd call."

I leaned back and closed my eyes. "Okay." I was too exhausted to argue or insist on anything.

Reluctantly, he let go of my hand. He fished his cell phone out of his pocket and punched in the numbers. I listened to Simon's side of the conversation without opening my eyes. My eyelids felt impossibly heavy.

"Lily, your mum wants to speak to you. If you're up for it."

I pried my eyes open and nodded.

Simon handed me the phone.

"Mom?"

"Lily," she sobbed, bursting into tears. I could hear Sir Richard's voice talking to her in the background as she cried. Then he came on the phone. "Lily, your mother is a bit overwhelmed at the moment. She wants you to know how relieved and happy we are. I'll be bringing her 'round to see you as soon as we get things sorted on our end."

"Okay," I said. I handed the phone back to Simon. He finished his conversation with Sir Richard and turned back to me. "I'll stay until your mum arrives. She'll want to have some private time with you." He watched me with a look of concern on his face. "Do you need anything?"

I licked my parched lips. "Water."

"One water coming right up," he said jauntily.

He returned a few minutes later with a plastic pitcher and a cup. He poured some water into the cup and handed it to me. "I know you are thirsty, but you want to take it slow."

I nodded and took several slow sips. "I'm in a hospital?" It was more a question than a statement.

"Right."

I was feeling so confused. "How did I get here? I don't remember anything about coming here."

Simon's mouth tightened into an angry line and his eyes darkened. "I'm not surprised. You were done in when we found you. Lord Yarlbury and I brought you here."

"Oh." I searched my memory but drew a complete blank. "You and Sir Richard? You found me?"

He nodded. His jaw muscle jumped as if he was clenching his teeth.

"How did you find me?" I asked.

Simon's expression darkened, but before he could answer there was a light knock on my door. We both turned to look as a nurse entered the room and smiled brightly at me. "I see you're up. That is good news. How are you feeling?"

"Better."

"Well, I expect so. You gave us all quite a scare when you arrived," she said cheerfully.

It seemed that I had given everyone quite a scare. Maybe it was a good thing I didn't remember anything.

Simon stood back to give the nurse room to work. She fussed with my IV, took my blood pressure and my temperature. After she left, two doctors arrived and did the same thing, except they also listened to my heart, and then asked me a bunch of questions. By the time everyone was done, I felt my eyelids growing heavy again. Simon must have sensed my exhaustion. He laid his hand over mine.

"Why don't you have a rest? I'll be here."

I nodded and sighed contentedly before closing my eyes. The nightmare was over. I was safe.

CHAPTER 31

RELIEF

December 11

Lily's hand felt cool in his. He watched her sleep and his heart jammed in his chest as he stared at the contrast of her dark lashes resting against the too pale skin of her cheek.

He told himself that she was going to be all right, although the terrible image of her crumpled form on the side of the road kept replaying in his head. That first sight of her had almost done him in. Watching her sleep, he still felt so bloody helpless. She looked so small and frail lying in the hospital bed.

He leaned over and brushed her lips with his. *She was all right*, he told himself. *She was going to be all right.*

The entire drive to the hospital, he had pressed her tightly against his chest, sharing his body heat with her, willing her back to life with every beat of his heart. He had to fight the urge to wrap his arms around her even more tightly when the medical staff appeared with the gurney to take her into the surgery. He watched in agony as they wheeled her into the Emergency Department, it was as if they had wrenched his own heart and lungs from his chest. He thought he would lose his mind waiting as the doctors worked on her.

But they had been lucky, very lucky. They had found her in time. The doctors said she would physically recover, and for that he was grateful. He suspected that the emotional healing, however, would take longer.

Lily twitched and let out a small cry in her sleep. Simon's face paled. Was she in pain? He gently squeezed her hand. She murmured something. His throat tightened. He leaned forward and gently brushed a loose strand of hair from her forehead.

"Where?" she murmured, moving restlessly.

Simon saw that her eyes were still closed. She was having a bad dream.

"It's all right, Lily," he whispered softly. "It's just a dream. I'm here. You're safe."

Her forehead creased with worry.

"Harry?" she murmured. "Harry?"

Harry? A ripple of jealousy snaked through him. Harry? Who the hell was Harry? She had never mentioned anyone named Harry to him.

"It's me, Simon. I'm here."

"Simon," she whispered.

"Yes, I'm here. It's all right."

She let out a little sigh and seemed to settle.

Relieved, Simon pressed the palms of his hands to his eyes. Harry? He must have misheard her. It had been a rough few days. He leaned his head against the back of the chair and closed his eyes. He could do with a bit of rest himself.

The next thing he knew, Lord and Lady Yarlbury were

standing in front of him.

He stood abruptly. "I didn't hear you come in. I must have dozed off."

"I don't wonder. It was a long night," Lord Yarlbury said.

Lily's mother stared anxiously at her daughter. "She looks so pale and thin. Are they sure she's all right?" She turned to look at Simon.

"Yes," Simon assured her. "The nurse was in before you arrived. She's just a bit done in, that's all. Once she rests a bit, she'll come around."

Her ladyship's eyes filled with tears. "Thank you, Simon. For everything."

"You look like you could use a cup of tea and a quick nap," his lordship said to Simon. "You're welcome to return to the flat to rest up if you like. Marguerite and I will hold the fort here."

Simon nodded. He understood. The room was far too small to accommodate the three of them and Lily's mum was going to want to have some family time with her daughter.

"That's very generous of you, but I think I'll pop over to my mate Paul's place. I've got my bag there."

His lordship placed a friendly hand on Simon's shoulder. "Thank you. We'll give you a ring once she's up and about."

"Right."

He left the hospital. Lord Yarlbury was right. He was done in. It had been a rough few days. He walked down the corridor, past the nurses' station to the elevator, and pushed the button, belatedly realizing that his car was still at Hampstead Heath. He took a quick look over his shoulder trying to decide if he wanted to walk back to Lily's room.

A loud ding announced the arrival of the lift. He shot a quick glance in the direction of Lily's hospital room but decided he didn't want to bother his lordship. He would find another way to fetch his car. He rode the elevator down to the ground floor, trying to remember the location of the nearest Tube stop.

It was still raining when he exited the hospital. He ducked under the entryway awning and bleakly contemplated the fat drops splattering the hospital walkway as he turned up the collar of his mac. He thought again about asking his lordship for a ride back to the heath. As he stood there, trying to decide what would be his best course of action, a taxi turned off the road onto the hospital drive.

No need to ask Lord Yarlbury. There was his answer. A bit pricey, perhaps, but well worth it.

Simon stepped forward to hail the driver, just as David Deene exited the car, ear pressed to his mobile phone.

"Where am I? I'll tell you where I am! I'm visiting my daughter in a damn hospital!" David Deene paused, listening intently for a moment as he climbed the steps. "No! We had an agreement and I expect you to honor it!" he shouted angrily as he hurried through the entryway doors, taking no notice of Simon.

Relieved to have avoided David Deene, especially after the incident at the embassy, Simon slid into the waiting car. He shook his head. *The man was all mouth and no trousers*, he thought. Lily was safe, but instead of being happy, her father was giving someone else aggro. He gave the driver directions to his car and leaned back against the seat.

CHAPTER 32

WHERE IS HARRY?

December 11

When I woke up, Simon was gone. My mom was now sitting in a chair by my bed. Sir Richard sat in a second chair across the room, reading.

"Lily!"

I scooted into a more comfortable sitting position. "Mom? Where's Simon?" I asked groggily.

"We sent him home to get some rest."

"Oh."

"He'll be back, sweetheart. Wild dogs couldn't keep him away." She smiled knowingly at me. "He was exhausted. I don't think he's slept since … well, since …" She reached over and held my hand. "So, how are you feeling?"

"Okay, I guess."

"Oh, sweetie." Her voice cracked.

"Don't cry, Mom. It's okay."

"It is now," she said.

I gave her hand a reassuring squeeze.

My mom's mouth trembled and she blinked rapidly. "Are you hungry?" she asked, rising abruptly to her feet. "I asked them to leave your dinner for you in case you were hungry when you woke up." She brought a tray over to me and set it on the bedside table. "I'm afraid it's going to be a little cold," she said, lifting the lid covering the plate of food.

"That's okay," I told her, although the thought of food made me feel slightly nauseous. I felt weak and shaky inside, kind of like when you get off one of those carnival rides that spins you around.

My mom adjusted the table and moved it so that I could reach the food.

I smiled weakly at her.

She gazed at me anxiously. "Do you need anything else?"

I shook my head. Skipping the cold meatloaf and roll, I ate a spoonful of the applesauce to make my mom feel better.

Sir Richard cleared his throat, peering at us over his half-moon reading glasses. "Why don't I fetch some tea?"

"Richard, that would be lovely," my mother said gratefully. "Thank you."

He raised an eyebrow in my direction. I nodded.

"Milk, no sugar, please," I told him.

"It shall be done."

That made me smile and Sir Richard winked at me. I do like Sir Richard. He is the most unflappable person I have ever met. Even something as disconcerting as a kidnapping didn't seem to upset him, which was nice since my mom could be, well, a little excitable.

After Sir Richard left, my mother fussed. She adjusted my pillows and asked me if I needed another blanket. She smoothed my hair. Was I warm enough? Did I want her to try and see if she could find someone to warm up my dinner?

"I'm fine, Mom. Really."

My mother sighed. "Oh, Lily. We were so worried. I'm so grateful that you are all right."

I leaned back against my pillow and closed my eyes. "Me, too."

"Your father stopped by earlier. You were still asleep. He asked me to let him know once you were awake. Do you want to give him a call? I'm sure he would like to hear from you."

"Can you call him?" I asked. "I'm not ready to talk to Dad right now." I knew that a chat with my dad would require more energy than I had at the moment.

"Of course, I can, sweetheart.

"I didn't realize he was in London," she commented as she looked for his number on her cell phone. "Did he tell you he was coming?"

I shook my head. "No. He just sort of stopped by."

"He flew all the way to London without even phoning first? Well, he certainly hasn't changed much," she said, working hard to keep her tone light.

I glanced over at her. "No, he hasn't."

She picked up a remote control from the tray table next to my bed. "Would you like to watch some television?"

"Sure."

She handed me the remote. "You're better with these things than I am."

I clicked on the television, pressing the mute button as I did so. I watched the silent images flicker past as I changed channels only half-listening to my mom's conversation with my dad. I could tell my dad wasn't pleased that I wasn't speaking with him. She finished her phone call.

"He's on his way," she said. "I'm afraid I couldn't put him off."

"That's okay. It's not that I don't want to see him, I'm just tired and Dad takes a lot of energy."

"Yes, he does."

We shared a little smile.

There was a soft rap on the door.

"Come in," my mother called.

Sir Richard entered carrying two steaming paper cups. He was followed by a small man wearing a suit and tie. At first, I thought he was another doctor.

Sir Richard handed one of the cups to my mom. The second cup he placed on my tray table. "Lily, this is Inspector Shah with the Metropolitan Police. He would like to ask you a few questions."

"Richard, is this really necessary? Now?" my mother asked. "She just woke up."

The police inspector smiled reassuringly at her. "Only if Lily is feeling up to it." He gave me a sidelong glance. "Do you feel well enough to answer a few questions? It shouldn't take long."

I nodded. "Sure."

"Good." He motioned to a young blonde woman wearing a police uniform standing in the doorway. "This is Constable Williams. She'll be taking notes for me during our interview." He looked at my mom and Sir Richard. "You are welcome to stay if you wish."

The small room was feeling decidedly crowded as Constable Williams apologetically squeezed inside.

"I don't think this is a good idea," my mother objected.

"It's all right, Mom. I'll be fine."

"Are you sure?" she asked, looking undecided.

"I am," I said with more confidence than I felt.

"Good. This won't take very long. May I?" Inspector Shah asked, gesturing to one of the chairs. I nodded and turned off the television.

He pulled the chair up to the side of the bed opposite of my mother and took a notebook and pen from his suit jacket.

"I understand you are a student at Kings Cross College," he said.

I nodded.

"I would like you to tell me about your school. Your mates, your courses, your activities. More or less everything you can recall about the last week before you were abducted."

I frowned at him, confused. "I don't understand. Why do you want to know that?"

"I would like to develop a sense of your usual routine. If we know your routine, it can help us to highlight people or situations that might have been out of place. What you may have thought was just a coincidence or unusual behavior might give us a clue to how your captors targeted you."

"Oh," I said, my voice suddenly sounding small and subdued. I cleared my throat and tried again. "Uhm. Where should I start?"

"I think it would be best to begin on Monday and work our way through the week," he said, smiling kindly at me. "Take your time."

I told him about my week. At least what I could remember about it. He asked a few questions like the names of my friends, what coffee shops I liked to visit, whether I had noticed anyone unfamiliar who might be loitering near my apartment or my classes, anyone who exhibited strange or unusual behavior, things like that. I couldn't remember anything unusual happening that week, other than my dad's surprise visit.

Inspector Shah cleared his throat. "Do you feel as if you could answer my questions about your abduction?"

At the mention of the word "abduction," I felt a jolt of adrenaline shoot through me, squeezing the air out of my lungs. My distress must have shown in my face because my mom reached over and squeezed my hand.

"If it's too much just now, you don't have to answer. Inspector Shah can come back another time," she said soothingly.

Inspector Shah glanced over at my mom, nodding

briefly. "Your mother is correct, but the more information we have, and the earlier we have it, the better our chances of apprehension."

I took a shaky breath. "It's okay. I can do it."

Inspector Shah asked me questions, leading me slowly and methodically through everything I remembered about the night I was kidnapped. It wasn't until we had finished going through everything that I suddenly remembered Harry.

"What about Harry? Did you ask Harry? Maybe he'll remember something."

"Harry?" Inspector Shah asked carefully, his eyes holding my gaze.

I nodded. "Haven't you interviewed him yet? He's not hurt, is he?" I looked quickly over at Sir Richard and my mother, searching their faces for information. I could see that they had no idea who I was talking about. I turned back to the inspector. "Is Harry all right?"

"I'm not sure I know who Harry is," he said. His eyes flicked toward my mom, who gave him a little shake of her head.

"Harry was with me." I glanced over at Sir Richard standing by the door. "Simon said you brought me to the hospital. Didn't you find Harry?" I asked, my voice rising.

"Find him where?" Sir Richard asked, confused.

"He was with me! He was right there with me! You left him there!" I started crying. "I can't believe you left him there!" Tears rolled down my cheeks at the thought of Harry alone in the cold and dark.

My mother squeezed my hand. "Lily," she said soothingly. "Richard and Simon found you on the side of the road. Alone."

I turned my tear-stained face to look at her. "On the side of the road?"

"Yes."

"But how …" I glanced up at Sir Richard.

"The …" he paused. "The man who called my mobile

gave us directions to find you."

I closed my eyes. "I don't understand," I said weakly.

"Lily," Inspector Shah interjected in a gentle voice. "The man who took you called your stepfather. That is how they found you. Was his name Harry?"

"No! Harry is my friend! He helped me!" I wailed. "Now he's alone!" I started to sob again.

My father chose that moment to arrive at my hospital room. As he stepped through the door carrying flowers and balloons, he saw me crying and two police officers sitting next to my bed. Of course, he jumped to the wrong conclusions.

My dad charged into the room thinking he was protecting me, shouting at Inspector Shah to get out of my room. Things got pretty messy after that. The inspector shot to his feet and tried to calm things down. Then my mom jumped in and tried to explain things to my father, but he kept yelling. That made Sir Richard angry, and then everyone seemed to be shouting at each other until a gray-haired, tight-lipped nurse banged the door open. It suddenly got quiet.

"This is a hospital, not a rugby pitch!" she barked angrily.

Inspector Shah immediately apologized. He took out his warrant card and introduced himself. "I am conducting a police investigation," he explained.

"Then I suggest you conduct this police inquiry quietly and appropriately or you will be escorted out of the building. All of you." She glanced around the room, her eyes steely. "Is that understood?"

Everyone nodded.

With a brisk nod, she turned on her heel and left, closing the door behind her.

"I would like to have a word with you lot," Inspector Shah told my parents and Sir Richard. "In the hall."

"Yes, of course," Sir Richard agreed quickly. He stepped over to the door and held it open, waiting for my mother.

She bent over and kissed me on the forehead. "I'll be right outside."

"Okay."

My mother stepped into the hallway. Sir Richard continued holding the door open as everyone looked at my dad. For a moment I was afraid he was going to refuse.

"You don't have to talk to them, you know," he told me. "They can't force you."

"I want to, Dad."

Finally, he reluctantly nodded. "Fine. Like your mother said, we're right outside." He cast a wary look at Inspector Shah before pushing past Sir Richard and stepping out into the hall.

The inspector turned to me. "I'll just be a few minutes. When I return, I'd like you to tell me everything you remember about Harry."

I nodded. Poor Harry. I couldn't believe he had been left behind. I vowed to do everything in my power to help the police find him.

After several minutes and a muted discussion that I couldn't quite hear through the closed door, Inspector Shah returned with Constable What's-Her-Name.

"I would like to continue our conversation, but your parents are going to wait outside. Are you comfortable with that arrangement?"

I nodded.

"Good. Now, tell me about Harry."

I tried, but there wasn't much to tell. I couldn't give him a description because I had never seen him. I didn't even know his last name. All I could tell him was how he helped me."

"He was foreign. I know that. He had an accent. I think he was German, but I'm not a hundred percent sure. He talked about someone named Rachel, but I don't know anything about her either."

Inspector Shah sighed. "Well then, why don't you tell

me everything you can remember about the place where they kept you and Harry?"

I shivered, remembering. "It was horrible. Cold and dark."

"Do you think you were in a house?"

I shook my head. "No. Harry said it was a bomb shelter. I think we were underground."

"A bomb shelter?"

"Yeah. That's what Harry called it. All I know is there were bricks on the floor and the walls."

"Windows?"

"No. No windows and one door, but it wasn't like a normal door."

"Can you describe it?"

"I'm not sure, I only saw it the one time when …" I caught my breath, remembering the man in the ski mask. "When he came and brought the cooler."

"When who came? Harry?"

"No! I already told you. Harry was there. In the dark, maybe in another place. I couldn't see him, but I could hear him. He would talk to me. I think maybe there was a vent or something. I don't know." I felt myself growing frustrated. "You have to try and find him. He said he'd been there for a long time. You have to find him!"

Inspector Shah's face was kind. "I will do my best. Is there anything else you remember about where you were?

"The ceiling was low. I could touch it. There were wooden beams on the ceiling and part of the shelter that had caved in. Bricks and dirt were on the floor. I think it was old."

"That's good. You are doing very well. Anything else? Strange noises? A peculiar light pattern?"

I racked my brain trying to think, but I couldn't remember anything that could help. I felt tears of frustration welling up in my eyes. I looked down and shook my head.

Inspector Shah's voice gentled. "It's all right. It's early

days yet. Something might come to you." He handed me his card. "If you remember anything else, you can call me."

I looked up and took his card. "But what are you going to do about Harry?" I asked.

He smiled reassuringly at me. "I'm going to contact Missing Person's Bureau to see if they can help me find a foreigner named Harry."

"Will you call me and let me know if you find out anything?"

"Absolutely."

CHAPTER 33

HOME SWEET HOME

December 15

Simon drove up the long gravel drive that led to Brynmoor Manor. The sun was setting, its last golden rays reflected in the mullioned windows, tinting gold the brick facade of the large estate. Each time he returned to the estate he felt the warm glow of home. He had grown up here in the gardener's cottage not far from the large manor house. His father still cared for the smooth lawns, precisely clipped hedges, and vast gardens of Lord Yarlbury's estate. His mum oversaw the day staff and maintained the manor house.

When he was younger, he had the run of the place. He, his sister, Jenna, and younger brother, Charlie, had made Brynmoor Manor their own personal playground. Charlie still did. His had been an idyllic childhood filled with long, lovely days in the countryside and tramps through the wood. Now that he was grown, his idyllic childhood had turned into a plot straight from a romance novel: the groundskeeper's son falls in love with the daughter of the English earl. He and Lily often joked about it.

He drove toward the stables and parked his car. He was worried about Lily. More worried than he let on. He knew from speaking with his mum this afternoon that he wasn't the only one.

"She's just not herself," his mum had told him. "It's to be expected of course, after what she's been through, but … well … she just seems … she's just not our Lily at all. Jenna's come 'round and it helps, but I think it's you she needs to see."

He got out of the car, closed the door softly, and walked to the stables. Once inside, he could see that the door to Posy's stall was open. Lily stood inside brushing the small horse. Posy, eyes half-closed, snuffled contently, enjoying the attention. Lily was so absorbed in her task that she hadn't noticed him approaching. He stopped and watched, quietly observing her.

His mother was right. The spark had gone out of her. She was pale, thinner, with dark bruises under her eyes, but it was more than that. She looked … He searched for the right word. Fragile. It wasn't a word he thought he would ever associate with her, but as he watched her, that was what came to mind. She looked impossibly fragile, as if she might shatter into a thousand pieces with a single touch.

Lily murmured soothingly to Posy as she stroked her, soothing herself as well, he thought. She sighed heavily and paused for a moment before pressing her forehead against Posy's sturdy shoulder, eyes closed.

Not wanting to intrude on her privacy anymore, he cleared his throat and called out her name. Startled, she jumped and let out a small squeak.

"Sorry," he apologized, striding toward her. "I didn't mean to frighten you."

Posy nickered happily upon hearing his voice. He stopped and rubbed Posy's muzzle, feeling strangely awkward as he stood beside Lily.

Her sad smile pierced his heart like an arrow. "It's not you. It's me. I'm a little jumpy these days. It's harder than I thought it would be to … to get back to normal." Tears welled up in her eyes and she blinked rapidly, turning away from him.

He reached out to her, touching her shoulder gently. "Lily, what can I do?"

She turned back around to face him. "Nothing. There's nothing you can do. It has to come from me. Oh, Simon, I'm afraid, and I hate feeling this way. It's not who I am. It's not who I want to be, but I am. I'm afraid all the time. I've started sleeping with the lights on. Isn't that ridiculous? I'm eighteen and I need a nightlight."

She stared up at him. The bleak expression on her face broke his heart.

"I have nightmares. If I don't leave the light on, I wake up thinking I'm back there. In that place." Her voice shook. "I thought being here, back at Brynmoor, would help, but it hasn't. Being here is making it worse. My mom hovers over me constantly. Everyone, your mom, Hudson, the rest of the staff … they all are walking on eggshells around me. No one jokes anymore." She swallowed hard. "My mom wants me to see a therapist, but I just want everything to go back the way it was."

Tears filled her eyes and rolled down her cheeks. The look of distress on her face was more than he could bear. Simon opened his arms and she slid into them. He held her close. "It's all right. It will be all right. It just takes time."

Simon's heart contracted painfully. He hurt for her. Lily was one of the most courageous people he knew. This was the same girl who had run into a burning building to save his little brother. The Lily he knew was equal parts stubborn and strong. She was a fighter. Someone had tried to take that from her. He made a vow to do whatever he could to help her fight her way back and help make her whole again.

CHAPTER 34

THERE'S NO PLACE LIKE HOME

December 15

Simon folded me into his arms. I rested my head against his broad chest and breathed deep, inhaling the scent of him as I listened to his strong, steady heart beating beneath his ribs. We stood wrapped in each other's arms for a long while. I clung to him, matching my breath to the slow rise and fall of his chest. I closed my eyes and let each beat of his heart and his every breath pull me steadily along like an ocean tide until it brought me to a calm, clear sea.

I had hoped that once I got out of that place, everything would be fine. I thought that I was having trouble sleeping at the hospital because I was in a hospital. Everyone feels anxious when they're in a hospital. I assumed that when I came back to Brynmoor, everything would be okay again, but being back here hadn't helped me at all. I felt hollowed out. It was as if the person I once knew as me was gone and there was nothing left behind but an empty shell. I needed to do something to make myself whole again. I just didn't know what I should do.

It didn't help that I felt a terrible lingering guilt about Harry. The police hadn't been able to find any information about him. I was here, safe at Brynmoor Manor, and Harry was still locked in that horrible dark place. The thought of it made me shiver. Simon's arms tightened protectively around me.

"What can I do?" he asked again.

I took a half-step back and looked up at him.

"I need to go to London." I hadn't known I was going to say that until it popped out of my mouth, but the minute I said it, I knew that it was exactly what I needed to do. I needed to go to London to find Harry.

Simon gazed down at me. "Why?" he asked, a faint worry line appearing in the space between eyebrows.

"Because I can't live like this. I don't want to be afraid anymore. I need to go back. I need to do something. I need to find Harry."

The expression on Simon's face changed. "Harry?" he asked carefully. "How are you going to find him?"

I sighed. "I'm not really sure."

"You're not sure?"

I shook my head. "No. I'm not, but I need to try. He saved me, Simon. I don't know how I'm going to do it, but I can't just abandon him. I have to help him, if I can. I need to go to London so I can at least try. I have to try."

"I understand that you want to help him, but you don't have any information to work with, not even a last name. How would you be able to find him?"

I sighed, thinking things through. Simon didn't say anything.

One of the wonderful things about Simon is his ability to listen. He really listens. Not just to your words, but to you, as a whole person. I think it's something he's learned working with animals. So, he didn't press me for an answer. He simply looked at me and waited patiently for me to explain.

"I know I don't really have any information, but I do know things about him," I told him. "For example, I know that he isn't English. I'm pretty sure that he's German. I'm not one hundred percent sure of that, but I think it's a pretty good guess. He spoke German to me the first time. When he spoke English, he had an accent. I know that the police think he was one of my captors, but they are wrong. He was a prisoner just like me. We were both there. We were both prisoners. I don't know what I would have done if he hadn't been there. He saved me." I looked up at Simon pleading with him to understand. "I owe him so much. I need to find him, or at least try my hardest to find him. I can't leave him there all alone."

"You really believe that the person who kidnapped you, also kidnapped this Harry person?"

I nodded.

"And you think you can find him?"

"I want to try. I need to try."

Simon nodded. "Right. Then we'd best find a place to sit down and see if we can come up with a plan to find him."

I nodded. "Okay."

Simon closed the door to Posy's stall, and we walked over to the tack room.

I sat on the short wooden bench next to the door. Simon turned over a feed bucket and sat on it, facing me. He reached over and took my hands in his, cradling them as gently and tenderly as if he was holding an injured baby bird. "All right, then. Tell me everything you can about Harry, and we'll try and get things sorted," he said.

I inhaled deeply. It felt so good to have someone listen, who was willing to believe me. I knew that whatever I said, Simon would give me the benefit of the doubt.

"He was there with me. In the …" I swallowed hard. Simon gave my hands a little squeeze.

"Take your time," he said. "I'm not going anywhere."

I smiled gratefully at him.

"He was in the room where they kept me. Kept us," I corrected. "He called it a bomb shelter. It was so dark, unbelievably dark. There was no light at all. We couldn't see each other or touch each other, but we could hear each other. He talked to me. I don't know, maybe there was a vent or something somewhere and that's why we could hear each other. I'm not sure what I would have done if I had been there alone. Just knowing that someone was there with me meant so much."

I realized that I was babbling, but I couldn't seem to stop myself. It was as if someone had uncorked a bottle. All of the thoughts and emotions I'd been trying to keep under control poured out of me.

"Harry saved me, but nobody believes me! He helped me and told me stories. He talked about his wife or maybe his girlfriend, I'm not sure. Her name was Rachel. So, we know there is someone out there named Rachel who knows who Harry is. He said he had been there a long time.

"Oh, Simon. I know that the police think he was one of the men who kidnapped me. Inspector Shah said they checked with Missing Persons, but I don't think they did. The doctors think that Harry was a figment of my imagination, that I hallucinated him. No one believes me, but I didn't imagine him! Harry is real! He is as real as you are!" I paused to catch my breath. "I need someone to help me, Simon. I have to try and find him, but I can't do it alone."

Simon's expression was thoughtful.

"You believe me, right?" I asked, knowing that I wouldn't be able to bear it if he didn't.

He nodded. "Yes. Yes, I do."

Simon believed me! It was as if a weight I hadn't known I was carrying had just been lifted from me. The world suddenly righted itself. I squeezed my eyes shut to keep from weeping with relief. "So, you'll help me? You'll take me to London?"

"Of course. I'll need to get things sorted at work, but we can probably go to London. I'll check with John."

"Thank you," I whispered, a tear escaping from the corner of my eye.

"Whoa," Simon said, releasing my hands and gently cupping my chin. He tenderly brushed the tear away. "What's this?"

"I don't know why I'm crying." I sniffed. "It's been happening a lot lately."

He studied me with a concerned expression on his face. "Well. Luckily for you, I know how to make you feel better."

"You do?"

"Absolutely. The Fitzgibbon cure for tears."

"I could use that," I said with a watery smile.

"This never fails. It's something my mum taught me."

"What is it?"

He leaned forward and tenderly pressed his lips to my forehead.

"Feel better?"

"A little," I told him.

He nodded. "I told you. It never fails."

"But I only feel a little better. I think I might need another dose? Right here." I touched my lips with my index finger.

Simon's lips twitched. "Hmmm. I think that can be arranged."

I can honestly report that the Fitzgibbon cure for tears works. By the time Simon walked me back to the manor, I was feeling a lot better. For the first time since I left the hospital I felt like my old self. I was on my way to taking control of my life again.

CHAPTER 35

A HEART ON THE WALL

1944
Hours Later

Once the door of their makeshift bomb shelter was closed, the thick brick walls muffled the noise of the air raid siren. The Hopley children quickly settled onto the floor, playing happily with their toys. Watching them was a welcome distraction. After twenty minutes or so the sirens stopped. Mrs. Hopley put down her knitting and walked over to the wooden cellar door, opening it a crack. As she peered out into the dark, they could hear the throbbing of the German airplanes as they passed overhead followed by the sharp staccato sounds of the anti-aircraft guns. She quickly closed the door, returned to her place on the bench, and resolutely began knitting again, her expression grim.

Heinrich sat in the cold and damp, waiting for the "all clear" siren to sound. Rachel rested her head on his shoulder. After another half hour, Mrs. Hopley's daughter told her children to pick up their things.

"It's time for bed," she told them. She turned toward her mother. "Mum, do you need another blanket?"

Mrs. Hopley shook her head. "I'm fine, dear. You look after the children."

"Do either of you children need to go to the loo before bed?"

The little girl made a face. "It's not a loo. It's a dirty old bucket."

"Well, when we are in the shelter it's our loo. So, do either of you need to use it?"

Both children shook their heads.

"Well then. It's time for bed."

"Do you mind if I turn down the lantern?" she asked Rachel as she tucked a blanket around the little boy.

"No. Go right ahead," Rachel replied.

Mrs. Hopley's daughter twisted the knob on the lantern until it emitted only a faint glow. She kissed her son on the top of his head before climbing onto the second cot and settling the little girl on her lap. The fact that fleeing your home in the dark to sit in a bomb shelter did not disrupt the domestic routine of families living in London struck Heinrich as strangely comforting.

Another hour passed. Heinrich stood, walked quietly over to the door, and pressed his ear against it. He would have liked to open it, but he didn't want to wake the sleeping children. He thought he could still hear the drone of the airplane engines followed by intermittent muffled bursts of gunfire. When he returned to their makeshift bench, Rachel looked at him questioningly. He gave his head a little shake. He noticed that one of the little girl's pastels had rolled under the bench. He reached down and retrieved it before taking his seat next to Rachel.

Rachel leaned her head against his shoulder again and sighed heavily. He knew she was thinking about their future separation. He was, too. The thought of leaving her filled him with an aching emptiness. He didn't want to go, but he knew he had no choice.

He gave her hand a little squeeze. She turned to look at him. Using the pastel he had picked up from the floor, he drew a lopsided outline of a heart on the brick wall.

Even in the dim light, he could see the glimmer of her smile. She plucked the pastel from his hand and, reaching across his body, wrote their initials inside the heart.

CHAPTER 36

RETURN TO LONDON

December 21

Simon put Lily's travel bag in the boot of his car and slammed it shut. It had taken him a few days to get things sorted at work, but John was being very accommodating about the situation with Lily. He wished he could say the same thing about his family. Last night, his dad had called him and given him an earful about carting Lily off to London when she should be home resting,

"What she needs is peace and quiet, walks in the gardens, time with her mum. Going to London isn't going to help her recover her health!" His father had barked angrily at the end of their phone call.

It made no difference to his family that Lily was the one who wanted to go to London. They were adamantly opposed to this trip. Even his sister, Jenna, had rung him to try and talk him out of it. Given all the fuss and bother, you would have thought he was forcing Lily to go to

London against her will rather than doing her a favor.

He could understand their concern. His family loved Lily, and seeing her look so frail and sad was difficult. It was difficult for him, too. Seeing her like that made his heart ache. The sadness was the worst. It was always there, even when she smiled, lingering just under the surface waiting to break free.

He wasn't certain that going to London was the right thing to do, but she thought it would help her and he trusted her instincts. He would do whatever it took to help her. Once she was strong again, he would find a way to deal with his anger. He wasn't a vengeful person, but this was different. This was about Lily. Someone had hurt her. If he ever found the person who did this to her, he was going to hunt him down and break him into a thousand pieces.

The front doors of Brynmoor Manor were open, and he could see Lily standing inside the Great Hall speaking earnestly to her mother. He opted to remain where he was. There was no way he was going to insert himself into *that* discussion.

He walked around to the driver's side of the car. Leaning a hip against the front fender, he waited. Unfortunately, he wasn't lucky enough to escape a last-minute scolding from his own mother. Unsmiling, she marched over to the car, a wicker basket in her hand. When she reached him, she paused and gave him the "look." He couldn't quite suppress the grin that creased his face. His mother had been using the "look" to bend her children to her will for as long as he could remember.

"It's no use you standing there grinning like a Cheshire cat, Simon Fitzgibbon. I think that the two of you haring off to London is nothing but foolishness. What our Lily needs is to be home with us taking care of her." She thrust the basket toward Simon. "I baked some scones and ginger biscuits. You make sure she eats in London."

Simon took the basket. "I will, Mum. Don't worry. I'll

take good care of her. I promise."

His mother looked up at her son, her expression softening a little. "I know you will."

He heard Lily call out, "Bye, Mom." Looking over the top of his mother's head, he watched her approach. She still had a bruised, frail look about her, but Simon thought he could detect a bit of the old Lily in the determined lift of her chin. She and her mum must have had words. She could be fiercely American when she was angry. The sight of that stubborn chin made him smile. Maybe this trip to London would be good for her. He hoped so.

Lily nodded at his mother. "Good morning, Mrs. Fitzgibbon."

"Good morning, my dear."

She turned to Simon. "Are we ready?"

"Your chariot awaits," he said with a small bow and flourish.

That brought a smile to her face. A real smile, one that reached her eyes.

He stowed his mother's basket in the back seat as Lily walked around to the passenger side of the car and got it in.

"Bye, Mum. Thanks for the scones and biscuits." He gave his mother a peck on the cheek before climbing into the car. With a jaunty wave, he started the engine.

Gravel crunched under the tires as they left the estate and drove toward the main road. Lily leaned back in the seat and closed her eyes.

Simon glanced over at her. "Had words with your mum, did you?" he asked.

"Yeah," she answered without opening her eyes. She breathed deeply, before glancing sideways at him. "Thanks for doing this for me, Simon. I know it wasn't easy for you to get out of work. I really appreciate it."

"You don't know the half of it. Work was the easy part. The family was another thing altogether. The entire lot gave me a good and proper tongue lashing."

The corners of her mouth tilted upward. "I know. Jenna called me. She isn't too happy with me either. She wanted us to wait so that she could come, too."

"What did you tell her?"

"I told her that I needed to go and talk to the police, and I didn't want to ruin my holidays, so we couldn't wait."

He glanced over at her, one eyebrow raised. "Did the police inspector ring you?"

She shook her head. "One of the police sergeants called to tell me that as far as they're concerned, Harry doesn't exist."

"Did he say that?"

"Not exactly, but that's what he meant. I think my mom probably called them and badgered them to call me. She doesn't want me going to London, but I have to go. If I don't look for him, no one else will."

"I believe you."

Her lips curved into a small smile. "I know. Have I mentioned lately how totally, unbelievably awesome you are?"

"Hmmm." He pretended to think about it. "I don't think so."

She sighed contentedly. "Well, you are. Pretty awesome, that is."

"Wow. Cheers for that. All this time I thought I was just pretty."

That got a little chuckle from her. It wasn't much, he thought, but it was a start.

Lily stretched her arm across the seat, palm upright. He laid his hand in hers and they turned onto the A5 and headed toward London.

CHAPTER 37

LOOKING FOR ANSWERS

December 21

I needed this trip. Not just to find Harry, but also to prove to myself that I could do this. I held Simon's hand, breathed deeply, closed my eyes, and let the music and the gentle thrum of the car engine lull me to sleep as we drove toward London.

I slept almost the entire two and half hours. I didn't wake up until we entered the city.

"Hullo, Sleeping Beauty," Simon said, flashing me a quick grin. "How are you feeling?"

I stretched. "Good." For the first time in days, I wasn't lying. I did feel good. Maybe it was my impromptu nap, or maybe it was because I was with Simon, but I felt good. Not great, but good. Good was a big improvement on how I'd been feeling since I'd woken up in the hospital a little over a week ago. Since leaving the hospital, I had become this timid, nervous person afraid of her own shadow and it made me both angry and ashamed. Ashamed at my own lack of courage and angry with the man who had made me feel this way. Traveling to London was my way of confronting my fears as well as helping Harry. I think it's a lot easier to be brave when you are fighting for someone besides yourself.

Simon pulled up to the curb in front of the apartment building and I hopped out to pick up a new set of keys from Osmin. Sir Richard, worried about my safety, had changed all of the locks for the flat.

Osmin greeted me with a wide welcoming smile. "It is good to see you again, Miss Lily."

"Thanks. It's good to be back. Though, I'm only staying for a few days. Simon is staying with me."

"Very good, Miss." He found the new keys and handed them to me. "It is a terrible thing that happened to you, Miss Lily. Everyone is very sorry." He shook his head, looking as distressed as if he had been personally responsible for what happened to me. "But I promised Lord Yarlbury. I will keep you safe. No one will get into the building when I am here. I promise you."

"I know you will keep me safe. Thanks, Osmin."

"If you need anything, you call me. Anything at all."

"I will."

"You take care, Miss Lily." He grinned.

"I will."

I hopped back into the car and Simon eased the car down the ramp and keyed in the code for the parking garage. We parked the car in Sir Richard's spot.

I felt the first flutters of anxiety as the doors to the elevator opened. I was returning to the flat, and I wasn't sure how I felt about it. I was also a little nervous about the elevator. Lately, one of my newly acquired phobias was a definite lack of comfort in small, enclosed places.

Simon shot me a worried look when I hesitated before entering the elevator. I straightened my shoulders and stepped inside. I kept my attention focused on the numbers as the elevator began to rise, counting off each floor in my head. When we reached the fourth floor, I exhaled sharply and stepped out into the hallway with a sense of relief. *Okay*, I thought, *I can do this*.

Simon and I walked down the hallway to Sir Richard's flat. I could feel my heartbeat quicken as soon as I fit the keys into the new lock. Pasting a cheery smile on my face, I turned to Simon. "Gentlemen first," I said, working to keep my tone light.

He gave me a quick sidelong glance. I wasn't fooling anyone with my little act, but Simon didn't say anything.

Simon pushed open the door as I hung back. He stepped inside. I waited a beat, then took a deep breath and crossed the threshold into the apartment.

"Do you want to put the groceries away or shall I?" he asked. His tone was casual, but I could tell by the way that he was looking at me that there was more to the question than just groceries.

"I don't mind. I'll put them away," I said, trying my best to hide my unease. "You can bring up the bags."

For a moment, I thought Simon was going to say something, but he changed his mind. "All right then. I'll put these in the kitchen for you."

I followed behind him, carrying my purse and the basket of goodies that Mrs. Fitzgibbon had made for us.

Simon deposited the bags on the kitchen counter and turned to face me, I felt a momentary flash of panic at the thought of being alone in the apartment. It must have shown on my face because Simon gave me a searching look.

"All right then?"

"I'll be fine." I managed a small smile. "Go ahead."

"I'll lock the door behind me. You can let me in."

I nodded.

I listened to the front door close and I stood in the center of the kitchen trying not to hyperventilate. I was alone in the apartment. Something I was going to have to get used to again. I silently reminded myself that I was safe. The locks had been changed. No one was going to be able to get in unless I let them in. Of course, there was that small niggling voice in the back of my head reminding me that the doors had been locked last time I was here, and it hadn't helped.

With my heart thudding anxiously in my chest, I glanced nervously at the front door. *There is nothing to be afraid of,* I told myself sternly. Inhaling sharply, I resolutely turned my back on the door and started unpacking the bags of groceries.

I had just finished putting the things away when I heard Simon knocking.

"Lily, I'm back."

"Coming!" I called out, a feeling of relief flooding through me. I folded the last bag and went to open the door for him.

"What did you put in this thing?" He puffed as he pretended to stagger into the room.

I couldn't help but laugh at his theatrics. I rolled my eyes. "Give me a break. It's as light as a feather."

"Light as a feather?" He grunted and dropped the bag to the floor with a resounding *thud.*

"Yes," I said, stooping down to pick up my bag.

He grinned at me. "Well then, since it's as light as a feather, why don't you carry it into the bedroom while I fetch the rest of the things from the hall?"

I crossed the living room carrying my bag. Thinking that maybe I had overpacked a bit. I opened the door to my bedroom and froze.

I was suddenly assaulted with memories from that night. I don't know what triggered them, but the memories came rushing at me like a high-speed train and knocked me flat.

I was immediately transported back to the night of my abduction. It's cold and dark. A man is here. In my room. I want to scream but he puts something over my mouth. I can't breathe. Sickly sweet taste and smell fill my mouth and nostrils. A sudden sharp pain in my arm.

I'm no longer sure if what I am seeing is real or not. My heart is pounding so hard that I think it might leap out of my chest. I can't seem to catch my breath. I am gasping and shaking so badly that I drop the bag. I hear the *thump* as it hits the floor, as if it is coming from some place far away. I try to open my mouth to yell, but no sound comes out. I need to move, but I can't. My legs crumble beneath me and I hear a terrible mewling sound coming out of my mouth as I curl into a tight ball trying to hide from the man in my room. I am crying and shaking so hard that I am not even aware of Simon returning.

Simon scooped me up and carried me to the couch.

"Shhh. Shhh. It's all right," he murmured as wet tears streamed down my cheeks. "It's all right. You are safe. I'm here. You are safe."

He wrapped his arms around me and rocked me like a little child as I curled into his chest, sobbing and shaking. Simon kept talking to me, his voice low and gentle. I imagined that I could feel his words on my skin tenderly stroking and soothing me, just as I felt his hands. Slowly, I came back to myself. I listened to the slow rumble of his voice. My heartbeat slowed and I stopped shaking.

I looked up at him, my face tear stained. "I'm sorry. I'm so sorry."

"Shhh," he soothed. "There's nothing to be sorry about. You've had a bit of a fright that's all."

I let out a shuddering breath and sat up. "I … I …" I wanted to explain, but I didn't have the words.

"Glass of water?"

I nodded.

"I'm going to go to the kitchen and get a glass of water. Will you be all right?" he asked.

I nodded again. I could see it in his eyes and the set of his jaw. *He's really worried about me*, I thought. "I'm okay," I assured him.

He gave me a long look before leaving me. When he returned, he brought me a glass of water and box of tissues. I blew my nose and drank the water, letting the coolness of it soothe my raw throat.

I swallowed hard and tried to explain. "It was like I was right there all over again," I told him. "I was standing there, and then all of the sudden it was happening to me all over again. He … he put something over my mouth, and I couldn't breathe. All I could smell was this awful sweet …" I gagged at the memory of that cloying smell.

"It's just a bad memory."

"I know, but it … it felt so real. I think my mom's right. I need a therapist. I'm seriously getting worried about my mental health." I buried my face in my hands.

Simon sat down next to me and placed his hands on my shoulders. "Look at me," he said.

I lifted my head.

"You've had a traumatic event and your mind is working through it. It's a normal reaction." He held my gaze. "The flight or fight response is hardwired into us, and when it's triggered by a traumatic event it can create very vivid memories. Seeing the bedroom triggered your memory and your body reacted with fear, just like it did when it actually happened to you."

I inhaled shakily. What Simon said made sense, but it was hard to accept.

"You have nothing to be afraid of," Simon said firmly. "You have to keep telling yourself that you are safe. I am not going to let anyone hurt you. The locks have been changed. No one is coming in here except you and me. You are safe. Keep telling yourself that."

"I know that. It's just …" I felt so ashamed. "Oh, Simon. I'm a mess."

He cupped my chin in his hands, forcing me to look at him. "No, you are not. You're feeling a bit wobbly right now, but you are going to get through this. You are stronger than you think. You are going to be fine."

"How can you say that?" I pushed his hands away. "I just had a panic attack in my own bedroom! Actually, I didn't even make it into my bedroom. I had a panic attack in the doorway of my bedroom. How am I going to live here if I can't even get into my own room?"

"You weren't prepared for it, that's all," he said. "It caught you by surprise, next time you'll be ready."

"Ready for what?"

"For the memory," he said. "Next time you are going to tell yourself that you are safe and that what you are feeling is just your body remembering fear."

I looked at him doubtfully. "I don't think it's that easy."

He smiled lopsidedly at me. "No. It's not easy, but I know you. I know you are strong. I know you are brave. I know you are going to be all right."

"I'm not feeling very brave and strong right now," I told him. "And I'm not sure I'm going to be all right."

"Just a bit of a setback. That's all. Things are going to get better."

"I hope so," I told him.

He leaned against the back of the sofa and pulled me toward him. I settled into the crook of his arm and rested my head against his shoulder. Wrapped in the protective cocoon of Simon's arms, I was almost ready to believe him. We sat that way for a while, content with each other's company.

The apartment phone rang, startling both of us.

"You don't have to answer that," Simon said.

"It's okay. It's probably my mom making sure that we've arrived. She called my cell phone, but my hands were full, and I didn't answer it."

I picked up the receiver. "Hello?"

It wasn't my mom. It was Osmin. My dad was outside and wanted to see me. My heart sank. I wasn't ready to deal with my dad just yet. Given the look on Simon's face when I told him who was downstairs, he wasn't either. I told Osmin to send my dad up, anyway.

"You can ask him to come back later, you know."

I shook my head. "No, I can't. My dad wouldn't understand." I managed a smile. "It's fine. I'm good."

Simon looked at me, eyebrows lifted doubtfully.

"No, really. I'm good," I assured him. "I'll just splash some water on my face, and we can have tea with my dad."

"Well, then I guess I'd better put the kettle on," Simon said.

CHAPTER 38

THE GAME IS AFOOT

December 21

By the time Simon finished making the tea tray, my dad was sitting in the living room with me. He looked up when Simon came in.

"Dad, this is Simon," I said, introducing them.

"We've met," my dad said in a flat voice, his expression cold and unwelcoming.

My gaze shifted between Simon and my father. "Oh."

Simon pasted a polite smile on his face. "I've made tea." He placed the tea tray on the sofa table.

"Was this your idea?" my dad asked Simon abruptly.

Simon paused. "Sir?"

I looked at my dad in surprise. "Dad, please."

My dad ignored me and addressed Simon. "This was your idea, wasn't it? Dragging her back here."

Simon shot me a quick sidelong glance. "I'm not sure what you mean."

"You know exactly what I mean! She shouldn't be here in London! She needs to rest, and if you really cared about her, you would turn around and drive back to her mother's right now."

"Dad!" I interrupted.

My dad turned to look at me. "Sweetheart. I'm sorry but he"—my dad jerked his head in Simon's direction—"does not have your best interests in mind."

"Dad!" I protested. "Coming to London wasn't Simon's idea, it was mine. I wanted to come back. Me. Not Simon."

My dad fixed me with a long look. "Why? Why would you want to come back here? You've just been through something that no one should ever experience. Your mom tells me you're not sleeping and that you're having nightmares. It is not a good idea for you to be here. You should be back with your mother resting and recovering."

"My college is here. I have to come back here eventually and finish up my exams from last term."

"I don't see why."

"Dad, they expect you to show up for class if you want a college degree. Even if I didn't come back to London now, I'd be back here in January," I told him.

"You can't possibly think that you're going to come back here in January. At the very least, you should take a leave of absence. You should stay with your mother in the country or transfer somewhere else. Someplace closer to home. Or better yet, you can come back to the states with me."

He nodded as he gazed at me, as if we had reached an agreement. "Yes. That's exactly what you need to do. You'll come to California with me. You can live with your grandmother and take some college classes. Then after things have settled, you can decide if you want to come back here or stay in California."

I felt a spark of annoyance light up inside of me. Who did he think he was? This man barely knew me, hadn't bothered to see me in years, and yet he suddenly thought he had the right to try and run my life.

"I am *not* going take a leave of absence. I am *not* going back to the states. I'm *not* going to transfer," I told him hotly. "I came to London to do something, and I'm *not* going to leave London until I decide to leave!"

Simon stirred next to me. I glanced over at him. He was trying, but he couldn't quite suppress the pleased expression on his face. I think he was relieved to see me standing up for myself, especially since I had been a sobbing wreck just a short while ago. Of course, my dad didn't share Simon's sentiments.

"What you need to do is rest and take care of yourself," he said, his voice adamant. "That is the only thing you need to do. There is nothing more important than that. If you don't want to come back to California, you should leave London and go stay with your mom."

I exhaled in exasperation. "Dad, I came to London to help Harry, and I'm not leaving until I do!"

"Harry? Who is Harry?"

"Harry was with me when I was … He saved me, and I am going to do everything I can to find him! I owe him!"

"Ah. That Harry." My dad's voice softened as he looked at me. "Tiger Lily, there is no Harry," he said with a sad little smile. "I know you think that he exists, but he doesn't. He was just a hallucination. A hallucination brought on by physical and mental stress. You've got to accept that."

"No," I said stubbornly. "I know that's what the doctors think, but they're wrong. Harry wasn't a hallucination. He is real. He does exist, and I am going to find him."

I could tell my dad was frustrated with me. He held his hands out, palms up. "How? Even if he does exist, how can you possibly find him? London is a big city with a lot of people living in it. If the police couldn't find him, why do you think you can? You don't even know where to start looking or what you are looking for."

"Dad," I began, but he held up his hand to stop me before I could protest any more.

"Listen to me, Lily. Even if this Harry person does exist, it's a wild goose chase. Frankly, this is not what you should be doing right now. You were released a little more than a week ago from the hospital. You need to rest, not spend your time running all over London."

I reached over and placed my hand on top of his. "Dad, I know you are worried about me, but I have to do this. I don't know how I'm going to find Harry, but I have to try. I owe to him and myself to try."

"I've brought a map of London," Simon interjected.

My father shot him an annoyed look.

Simon continued undeterred. "I've marked the two locations we know about. I thought we could start there."

I gazed at Simon, my heart swelling with love and gratitude. I would have kissed him if my father hadn't been sitting across from us. "See, Dad! Simon has a plan. It's going to be fine. We'll use the map and start a search pattern."

"A search pattern for what? What exactly are you going to be looking for?" he said, shooting another look Simon's way.

Simon shrugged. "We know where we dropped off the money and we know where we found Lily. We'll start there."

"Start by doing what?" my dad asked with a shake of his head. "Driving around London hollering 'Harry' out the car window? That's not only ridiculous, it is dangerous." He inhaled deeply, started to say something, then stopped himself. Softening his voice once again, he took my hand in his. "Lily," he began. "Look, if you really believe that this Harry exists, then the best way to find him would be to let the police do their job. They have resources that you don't have and it's what they are paid to do. Let them do their job. Your mother and I both agree that the best thing for you to do would be to take some time to allow yourself to heal."

He shifted his gaze to Simon, his eyes narrowed. "And you, if you cared for my daughter, you would not be encouraging this wild goose chase."

"Dad, I'm not going back!"

Seeing the expression on my father's face made me feel guilty for yelling. After all, he was just saying those things because he was worried about me.

I lowered my voice and tried to explain. "Dad, I want you to understand. I have to try. I have to do this because no one else will. The police don't believe me about Harry. So, you can either help me or leave. I'm sorry, Dad, but that's the way it is. I'm not leaving London until I've done my best to find Harry."

My father sat back and sighed heavily. "You are so stubborn," he said finally.

"Yes, I am," I agreed. "So, are going to help me, or are you going to leave?"

"Of course, I'll help you."

I felt a slow smile spread across my face. "Really?"

"Really. On one condition."

I waited expectantly.

"You will not do anything foolish or dangerous."

"I won't," I promised. "Thanks, Dad."

"All right, Tiger Lily. What do you want me to do?"

Simon cleared his throat. "Lily said she was held in a bomb shelter. Which means, most likely, the building was built during or before World War II. I thought we might make a list of addresses of older buildings, starting with the two locations I marked on the map. From there we can form a search pattern."

I gazed adoringly at Simon. "That is positively brilliant," I told him.

The corners of Simon's mouth twitched. "All in a day's work," he said smugly.

I looked over at my dad. "See, Dad. Now we have a

definite plan."

"Yes. I can see that. You two are a regular Sherlock Holmes and Watson."

I ignored my Dad's sarcasm and turned toward Simon. "Well done, Watson."

"Watson? I just came up with the plan. Doesn't that make me Sherlock?"

"Only if you solve the case," I quipped.

He grinned. "Well, then I'd better get my laptop. After all, the game is afoot."

We set up our command center in the kitchen. I searched Google Earth while Simon tackled the London Housing Registry and my dad compiled our list of potential addresses, cross-checking them with real estate listings. I was pleased that Simon and my dad established a kind of a mutually agreed truce. While the two of them weren't acting like best friends, at least they were no longer openly hostile to one another.

As we worked, we drank tea and ate Mrs. Fitzgibbon's ginger biscuits. It felt really good to be doing something.

After a couple of hours, my dad glanced down at his watch. "Hey, Tiger Lily, I can't stay much longer. I've got a dinner meeting in an hour. I'm afraid I've got to get going."

I looked up and stretched, rolling my neck. "That's okay, Dad. Simon and I can take it from here. Thanks for all your help."

Simon didn't say anything.

"Why don't I take a look at some of the addresses on the list after my meeting? That way you won't have as many to look at tomorrow," he suggested, his gaze sliding over Simon as if he wasn't there.

I glanced over at Simon. "What do you think?" I asked him.

He looked up from the computer briefly, keeping his

expression carefully neutral. "It's up to you."

"Uhm, okay. Sure," I told my dad. "That would be great."

My dad shuffled through the papers. "I organized the addresses by street location so it would be easier to plan a search," he said. He picked up a sheet of paper. "I can take these," he offered. "They're close to my meeting tonight, so I can run by and check on them after dinner."

I glanced over at Simon again. He stared fixedly at the computer screen, not willing to engage with my father.

I shook my head in exasperation at both Simon and my dad. The two of them were behaving like children. "That's fine," I told my dad. "I'll walk you to the door."

I gave my dad a hug and he left. When I returned to the kitchen, Simon was closing his laptop. His mood had definitely lightened now that my father was gone.

"I need to eat something besides ginger biscuits," he said. "Let's take a break and find some real food." As if to emphasize the point, his stomach grumbled.

We both laughed. "Chinese?" I suggested.

He shook his head. "No. I'm starved. Chinese isn't going to do it. Fish and chips?"

I made a face. "Pizza," I countered.

"Sausage topping?"

I grinned. "Half sausage. Half vegetarian."

"Deal."

I wanted to order takeout so that we could keep working, but Simon insisted that we leave the flat and go out. "I need a break and so do you," he said firmly. "The fresh air will do us good. It will help stimulate our brains."

I rolled my eyes but agreed.

I have to say that Simon was right. It was good to take the break. I felt energized after our pizza and ready to go back at it as soon as we returned to the flat.

"Okay. Let's get back to work."

"You're the boss." Simon sighed, following me into the kitchen. "Why don't we move into the living room?" he suggested. "If I have to keep working for the next few hours, I'd rather settle my bum on that very cozy sofa than sit for another hour on one of these kitchen chairs."

"All right," I agreed, giving him a playful pat on his very attractive bum.

He was right. It was more comfortable. We ended up working for a couple more hours.

A little after 10 p.m., Simon leaned back, rested his head against the back of the sofa, closed his eyes, and exhaled theatrically. "Lily, I'm knackered," he said. "Let's call it a night."

I glanced nervously at the bedroom door. The thought of walking into that bedroom again made my stomach churn. If I couldn't walk into it in broad daylight, how was I going to do it now when it was dark outside? I couldn't guarantee that I wouldn't have another weird flashback and break down again.

"Uhm. You go ahead. I want to finish up a little more," I told him.

"Are you sure?" he asked. "You look all in."

I shot another glance at the bedroom. "Yeah." I nodded. "It won't take me very long, but you don't need to wait up for me. I'm not tired yet."

The "not tired" part was a total lie. I was exhausted. Unfortunately, there wasn't much I could do about it. Sleeping had become a problem for me ever since I left the hospital, and sleeping in the dark was … well, it was a bigger problem.

Simon studied me with a thoughtful expression on his face. I knew I wasn't fooling him, but he didn't try and force the issue.

"All right, if that's what you want," he said. He stood and stretched, yawning loudly, before disappearing into the bedroom.

I berated myself for being such a wimp. Tomorrow, I told myself. Tomorrow, I'll go into the bedroom. I stared at my computer screen, rubbing my eyes as I forced myself to focus on the house listings and tried not to think about being alone in the flat. I glanced involuntarily at the front door to assure myself for the hundredth time that it was locked and reminded myself that Simon was in the next room.

I sighed and began reviewing addresses. I could hear Simon moving around the bedroom as he unpacked. After a few minutes, he came out of the bedroom carrying a pile of blankets and two pillows.

I looked up. "What are you doing?"

"Never mind me, you keep working," he said with a wink.

Of course, I couldn't help but "mind" him. I watched as he dropped the blankets and pillows on one of the armchairs. Next, he moved the armchairs, shifting them farther away from the sofa and turning them so that the seats faced away from each other. He took one of the blankets and shook it out. Then he spun around and with a flourish worthy of any Spanish bullfighter, draped the blanket over the two chairs forming a canopy. He paused, grinning at me as I stared up at him open-mouthed.

"Thought we'd have a bit of a campout in the living room," he said, his eyes laughing. "Behold! Our tent," he said, indicating toward the chairs and blanket with a theatrical sweep of his arm. You can join me when you're ready."

I laughed aloud, my heart swelling with love for him. "You are insane."

"Mad as a box of frogs," he agreed. "Mad as a box of frogs *about you*," he added softly.

My throat squeezed tight with emotion as I thought about how incredibly lucky I was to have found someone like Simon.

He shook out the rest of the blankets and laid them on the floor, tossing the pillows on top of them. When he was finished, he stood back surveying his makeshift tent with a critical eye.

I closed my laptop and went to him. "It's a lovely tent," I said. "Thank you."

He looped one arm around my waist. "Not half bad, if I do say so myself." He pulled me toward him, and I wrapped my arms around his neck.

"I think it's supposed to rain tonight," I teased.

"I guess we'll just have to take our chances," he murmured, resting his chin on the top of my head as his arms tightened around me.

I sighed contentedly and snuggled closer, enjoying the feel of him. "You know," I told him, eyeing the blankets on the floor. "You would be more comfortable sleeping in the bed.

He pressed his lips to my forehead. "Yes, but I would be lonely," he said is voice husky.

I felt a little jolt of electricity shoot from the top of my head and down my spine. It made my whole body hum. I smiled up at him. "Well then, I guess I'd better help you finish setting up our camp.

CHAPTER 39

A PICNIC IN THE DARK

1944
Summer

He slept in abandoned buildings, making sure to move to a new location every few days. It was a miserable existence. Once again, he had become a shadow walking among his fellow human beings. Food was scarce. Without ration cards, it was almost impossible to find enough food to sustain himself. In order to survive, he had taken to scavenging the rubbish bins behind the luxury hotels for whatever bits and crusts the rich and famous had left on their plates.

Worse than the hunger, though was the loneliness. The absence of Rachel was like a constant hollow ache under his breastbone. He found that despite his best intentions, he couldn't make himself stay away from her.

He began following her as she walked to and from the hospital. He lived and died for those evenings when he would trail behind her, hiding in the shadows, his eyes on her crisp white nurse's cap and dark blue cape as she made her way through the streets of London. Sometimes it was all he could do to keep from calling out to her.

One evening he followed her as she walked past the alley where they first met. He heard a voice call out and watched as she stopped short. She hesitated and peered into the alley, a look of hopeful expectation lighting up her face. "Harry?" she called.

"Who yer looking for, duckie?" a drunk soldier slurred as he staggered out onto the street smiling sloppily at her.

Startled, Rachel gasped and hurried away, tears in her eyes.

The soldier stumbled after her. "Whash yer hurry?"

Heinrich stepped out of the shadows, blocking his path. The soldier swayed on his feet and blinked in surprise at Heinrich's sudden appearance. After a moment, he saluted Heinrich, then slowly turned and trundled off in the opposite direction.

Heinrich hurried after Rachel. He watched as she stopped in front of the hospital. She leaned against the iron fence and buried her face in her hands. Seeing her weep sliced through his heart like a dagger. Knowing that she wept because of him was almost more than he could bear. He had to explain. He couldn't let her think that he had abandoned her. He had just decided to speak to her when another nurse arrived. He quickly retreated.

"Rachel!" The second nurse exclaimed, alarmed.

Rachel's reply was muffled. She wiped her eyes.

Heinrich watched as two women spoke. Heads bent together, they entered the hospital building.

That night he slipped a note into Rachel's letter box. On a scrap of paper, he drew a heart inscribed with their initials and the word *Tonight.*

He waited and watched with anxious anticipation as she retrieved her mail the next day. Mr. Blackthorn stopped at the letter box and he and Rachel exchanged pleasantries.

She looked at the paper. Heinrich couldn't see the expression on her face, but after she read it, she stole a quick look up and down the street.

Mr. Blackthorn said something to her. She smiled politely and shook her head as she quickly folded the paper and slipped it in her pocket, pausing on the front steps to scan the street once more before disappearing inside.

Blackout curtains were being drawn across windows as Heinrich left the abandoned warehouse, he had been calling home for the last two nights. He walked the London streets feeling almost giddy with anticipation. When he finally arrived at Rachel's street, he paused, surveying the building to make sure that none of her neighbors were out and about and waited for Rachel.

It was fully dark when the front door opened. For a brief moment, Rachel stood on the front step illuminated by the hall light before she quickly pulled the door closed. In the dim moonlight, he could just make out her silhouette. She paused for a moment, waiting for her eyes to adjust to the darkness before carefully feeling her way down the steps.

A yellow half-moon cast its faint light across the night sky. There was just enough light for him to follow her progress as she made her way around the side of the house to the back garden. Sliding through the front gate, he followed her. She walked quietly, a shadow moving among shadows. Even if one of the neighbors saw her, they would not be able to identify her with any certainty.

She descended the steps to the bomb shelter. He waited and watched for another ten minutes. All was quiet. Then he also made his way down the steps leading to the shelter. He pushed opened the door and peered inside, unable to see anything in the dark interior.

"Rachel?" he called softly.

"Harry? Is that you?"

"Ja. I will close the door then you light the lantern."

He pulled the door closed and waited. She flicked on her torch and used it to locate the lantern. She lit the wick and set the lantern on the bench. She gazed at him unhappily. The smile he wore faded. He crossed the room, feeling strangely hesitant.

"You left," she said, looking up at him, a frown on her face. "You left without telling me. I woke up and you were gone."

He could feel her anger and hurt as if it were a real thing hovering in the air between them. His knees suddenly went weak with fear that she would send him away.

"Rachel, I had no choice," he said, standing before her. "I did not want to leave. I had no choice. It isn't safe for you. I left to keep you safe."

Her head snapped back angrily. "You didn't even say good-bye."

Her voice caught in her throat and before she turned away from him, he saw the glimmer of unshed tears.

He knelt before her. "I am sorry that I hurt you, but you cannot know where I am. It isn't safe for you to know. Please, Rachel. Do not be angry. I left to keep you safe."

She turned to face him once again. "My uncle—"

He cut her off before she could finish what she wanted to say. "No. I will not put your family in danger. This is the only way."

"But what will happen to you if they find you?" She looked up at him, her voice trembling.

"They will not find me." He reached for her and pulled her to her feet, wrapping his arms around her. He buried his face in her hair and breathed her in. He felt the anger and tension go out of her. She squeezed him tightly.

"You are too thin," she said, stepping back from his embrace. "Sit down. I brought you something to eat."

He had been so focused on Rachel that he hadn't noticed the small picnic basket she brought with her.

Heinrich grinned happily, drinking in her every movement as she set out a picnic of bread, cheese, and cider. She sliced some cheese and placed it on the bread, handing it to him. He forced himself to chew slowly as she watched him eat with a critical eye.

The muffled wail of the air raid sirens sounded.

Heinrich stood abruptly. "That is the siren. I must go before the others come."

Rachel reached out, grabbing his hand to detain him. "No. You don't have to leave."

"But they will find us here."

She shook her head. "No, they won't. We are not using this as a shelter anymore. We are all supposed to go to the Anderson shelter now."

"There are too many people for one shelter."

She smiled. "Not anymore. Mrs. Hopley left with her daughter and the children to Southbourne. They are going to stay with her sister. We can stay here tonight. The others will go to Anderson shelter. No one will find us."

Heinrich glanced worriedly at the door before sitting down again. "You are certain?"

She nodded. "Yes. Tonight it will be just the two of us."

Heinrich glanced worriedly at the door.

"I promise." She opened a bottle of the cider and poured it into two glasses. She handed him a glass. "Harry, there is something I have to tell you," she told him, her expression grave.

He carefully set his glass on the wooden bench and turned to give her his full attention.

"They are closing the hospital."

"Why?"

"With the new German offensive, they don't think it's safe. The new building isn't big enough for all of the patients they expect, and they don't think it is safe to keep patients in one building because of the increased bombings. They are moving the patients who can travel out of the city. The ones who can't travel will be transferred to different clinics or homes."

"And you? What will you do?"

"I am leaving London." Her mouth trembled. "I'm sorry. I was angry with you. I didn't know where you were or if you were still in London. I called my father. He had found me a job in Oxfordshire. I'm sorry. I ..."

"Shhh." He gently pressed a finger to her lips. "It is good for you to go. London is not safe. You will be safe with your family."

"But what about you? It's not safe for you either. You should go and work on my uncle's farm."

He shook his head. "It is better for me in the city. There are many people here and it will not be so easy to find me. If I go to your uncle's farm, people will notice me. They will know that I am foreign, and they will ask questions."

"But we can tell them—"

"No," he interrupted her. "This is not safe for your family. This I will not do," he said firmly. "When do you leave?" he asked.

"Two weeks." She turned to him, her eyes filling with tears once more. "I am afraid, Harry. What if we never see each other again?"

"That will not happen. We made a plan to meet after the war."

"I know, but what if I can't find you when the war is over?"

He grinned at her. "You will find me because when the war is over, I will be here." He patted the bench, then gestured to the chalk heart they had drawn on the bricks. "Waiting for you."

CHAPTER 40

THE NIGHTMARE

December 22

They lay on the floor nested together like two spoons. Simon draped an arm across Lily's waist and closed his eyes, listening as her breathing deepened and slowed. She was going to be all right, he told himself. It would take time, but she was going to be all right. She was growing stronger every day. He could see glimpses of the old Lily fighting to break out like sunbeams peeking through heavy clouds. Today, when he saw that very familiar stubborn lift of her chin and watched her stand up to her dad, he had almost shouted with joy.

She was such a tantalizing combination of tenderness and fierceness, fearlessly meeting anyone or anything head-on in order to help someone in need. Her strength of spirit and finely honed sense of fair play were two qualities that he admired about her. Which was why he had almost come undone when he found her curled up on the floor, shaking and sobbing in terror. Seeing her like that tore him to pieces. He felt anger rise once again, curdling in his belly at the thought of the person who had done this terrible thing to her. This person had ripped Lily's safe and secure life apart and destroyed her confidence. The worst part of it was that there was nothing he could do to make it right again.

Beside him, Lily whimpered, and her body arched in protest as he unconsciously tightened his arm around her. He relaxed his arm and pressed his lips to her hair. "It's all right," he murmured. "I'm here. Go back to sleep."

She sighed in her sleep and he felt her body go lax again.

"There you go. Just close your eyes and sleep," he soothed as he nestled closer to her and closed his eyes, drawing in a long slow breath. Later, he promised himself. Later he would find some way to deal with the anger that was clawing at him. Right now, he had to push it away and focus on taking care of Lily because that was what was most important.

He woke with a start. Lily's body was rigid with fear and she cried out in her sleep.

"Lily?" he said softly, reaching out to her. When his hand touched her, she flailed in panic, striking him hard in the face and shouting in fright as she bolted upright. He tried to hold her, but she struck him again, clawing at him in her terror. He winced and grabbed her arms to keep her from hitting him again.

She stared at him unseeingly, eyes wide with terror, struggling as he gripped her firmly.

"Lily," he said again. "It's all right. You're safe. It's all right. You're safe."

His words finally cut through her panicked dream state and she stilled, breathing fast and hard.

"It's all right," he repeated. "It's me. Simon."

"The lights," she gasped. "You turned off the lights."

"Ah. Right. Hold on." He scrambled to his feet and hurriedly turned on the table lamp next to the sofa. "There you go. Do you need more light?"

She shook her head. Her eyes were wide with fright. She was shaking. "I … can't … breathe …"

He looked directly at her, holding her gaze. "Yes, you can. You're just breathing too fast and too shallow. Breathe with me. Inhale and hold it. Long, slow breath out. Inhale deep and hold it. Long, slow breath out." He watched as the panic let go of her. "That's the way of it. Smooth and steady."

The trembling ceased. The color came back into her face. Her breathing returned to normal.

"Wow," she said weakly.

"You're all right?" he asked.

She nodded.

He leaned in and touched his forehead to hers. "You're cold. I'll get you a blanket and your robe. Are you going to be all right, if I go get them?"

She nodded again.

He crossed into the bedroom, noticing in surprise that his hand was shaking as he pulled the extra blanket and her robe from the closet. *No wonder*, he thought. He'd just had a rather large dose of adrenaline dumped into his system. He stood for a moment and breathed in deeply, searching for calm. He would need to be calm to help Lily.

The intensity of her nightmare had caught him unprepared. She had been so completely in the grip of her dream that she hadn't even known who he was. He had never experienced anything like that before. He exhaled slowly and returned to the living room.

"Here you are," he said gently, draping the blanket around her shoulders before sitting on the floor next to her. "I've got your robe if you want it." He held it up.

She shook her head. "I'm good."

"Bad dream?" he asked.

She nodded.

He reached for her hand. She was still trembling. "Do you want to tell me about it?"

"More of the same," she said dully. "Someone puts a cloth over my mouth, and I can't breathe. I try to fight him, but I can't breathe." She paused and gave his hand a little squeeze. "The dark makes it worse. I wake up and I can feel the dark filling up my nose and mouth, getting into my lungs, cutting off my breath."

She turned to look at him and her eyes widened in horror. "Oh, no! Did I do that?" she asked, staring intently at Simon's face.

"Do what?"

She reached up and gently touched the side of his face. He winced.

He gingerly felt along his cheekbone, feeling the raised scratch marks. "I guess you did."

"Let me get a cold cloth for you."

"It's fine."

"No. Let me do this. Please." She jumped up and ran into the bathroom. Simon could hear the water running. She returned with a wet washcloth and kneeled beside him. Gently she dabbed the cloth over his face. "Simon, I'm so sorry. I think you are going to have a bruise."

He grinned at her. "Well, I always tell people that I was gobsmacked when I met you."

"It's not funny," she said, looking at him unhappily. "I hit you. I am so sorry, Simon. I thought he was back. I thought you were trying to …" She sighed heavily. "God! I'm a total mess. I thought that with you here, I wouldn't be afraid, that I wouldn't have nightmares, but I was wrong."

"The nightmares are the way that your mind is trying to sort through the bad memories and process them. Perhaps it wasn't a good idea to come to London so soon. Perhaps your mum was right, and we should go back to Brynmoor."

"No!" She shook her head. "I need to be here. I need to do this. Not just for Harry, but for me." She looked up at him, her eyes pleading. "Please. I don't want to leave yet. Give me a chance. Just a few more days."

Simon gazed at her, his expression somber. "All right then. We'll stay. Tell me what I can do to help you."

She sat back on her heels and gave him a sad little smile. "Nothing. This is something I have to do for myself." She gave her head a little shake. "I don't want to be afraid anymore. I don't want to be a victim for the rest of my life."

"You won't be," he assured her. "It's just going to take time."

"I know. Everyone keeps saying that. Over and over and over. The problem is that I've never been very patient. Coming to London is me trying to find a way to get back to who I am." She looked into his eyes and it was all he could do not to gather her up in a crushing embrace and comfort her, but he knew that this wasn't the right time. He wished he could take away the bad dreams and memories, but he couldn't, and it made him feel so bloody helpless.

"Do you know what the worst part of this whole thing is?" she continued. "The worst part is not knowing why. Why did this happen to me? I don't know why he picked me, and because of that I don't know how to protect myself. I keep thinking that if I knew who he was, then I would know why he kidnapped me." She inhaled deeply, lifted her chin, and squared her shoulders. "I am not going to let him win. I won't let him make me a victim."

"Well done," he told her. "You keep fighting, Lily and I'll be right here with you every step of the way."

With a ghost of a smile, she reached out and tenderly traced her fingers along his bruise. "I'm counting on it," she told him. "Though it might be a good idea for you to learn a few more self-defense moves."

He caught her hand and brought it to his lips. "Do you

know how extraordinary you are?"

"What?"

"Extraordinary. You are extraordinary, amazing, and brilliant."

"What are you talking about?"

"You. You are the bravest, most courageous person I know."

She looked at him in surprise. "How can you say that? I'm not brave. I'm afraid. I'm terrified. I was so terrified that I hyperventilated and punched you in the face. We've only been here one day, and I've already had two panic attacks. I'm not brave at all."

"That's not true," he said firmly. "You are brave. You came back to London. You tried to go into your bedroom. You could have chosen to hide at Brynmoor, but instead you've come back to London. You're frightened, but you aren't letting that control your life. You are here, confronting your fear, and that is what makes you extraordinary."

The corners of her mouth turned up. "So, I'm brave and afraid at the same time?"

He brushed his lips against her forehead. "Yes."

She gave her head a little shake, scooting closer to him. "Thank you for staying with me," she said, gathering the blanket around her shoulders like a cape. "And thank you for believing me. About Harry, I mean."

"I know better than to argue with a girl who can paste a bloke nearly twice her size," he said with a grin as he gingerly patted his bruised face.

Lily didn't return his smile. "Does it hurt?"

"Terribly," he said, his expression serious.

"It does?"

He nodded. "Yes, but I think a kiss would make it feel much better." He pointed to his cheekbone. "Right here."

The corners of Lily's mouth turned up. "I thought the Fitzgibbon cure only worked for tears."

"Oh, no. It's an all-purpose cure. It works for bee

stings, skinned knees, and all manner of bumps and bruises," he told her solemnly.

"Well then, let me see what I can do."

She reached up and gently pulled him toward her, grazing his face tenderly with her lips. "How is that? Better?"

"I think I could use a bit more. Perhaps here and here," he said, touching his jaw and chin with his finger.

Lily dropped the blanket from her shoulders and leaned forward, planting a kiss on his jaw and another on his chin. "Better?"

Simon cleared his throat. "Much better. Perhaps we should try to get back to sleep," he said huskily.

Lily smiled at him. "Oh, I wouldn't recommend that. You are definitely going to need more of the Fitzgibbon cure before you can go back to sleep."

CHAPTER 41

DOODLEBUGS

1944
Fall

With Rachel gone to Oxfordshire, Heinrich moved into their former bomb shelter. He rationalized that he was safer here than he would be sleeping above ground, especially now that the Germans had increased the number of bombing raids on London. The German *Luftwaffe* had invented yet another killing weapon, a new type of bomb propelled by its own engine. This new bomb could be launched from miles away, keeping the German pilots a safe distance from London's anti-aircraft gunners. With little risk to their pilots, the German bombing raids were limited only by their supplies of planes, bombs, and petrol, which meant that London was under constant siege.

Perhaps as an attempt to make the new bombs less frightening, the British had nicknamed them "doodlebugs," as if they were some harmless type of insect. Whether you called them German V1 rocket-propelled bombs or doodlebugs, Heinrich thought, it did nothing to change the devastating destruction they left in their wake.

The first V1 rocket attack was launched by Germany on June 13th. Heinrich heard the new bombs before he saw them. He had been returning from spending the last of the ration cards that Rachel left him. As he walked along the street, carrying his bread and cheese, he heard a dull coughing sound overhead. Looking skyward, he noticed what appeared to be a parade of slim black fountain pens with wings flying above him in a bright blue sky.

It had been a shock when the fountain pens began to drop on the city. As Hitler's V1 rocket bombs landed, the concussive blast was like nothing anyone in London had experienced before. The warheads exploded on impact, creating a huge fireball, flattening entire buildings in seconds, and bringing instant death and destruction to everyone and everything in their vicinity.

During the war, everyone in London had become used to nighttime bombing raids, but these bombing raids were different. The deadly doodlebugs arrived during the day. It was unnerving. You never knew when one might drop from the sky.

Sometimes your first warning of a bombing raid was a distinctive coughing, whirring sound overhead. As soon as you heard them, you stopped what you were doing, turned your face skyward, and listened. As long as you heard the drone of their engines, you knew you were safe. It meant they were going to fly past and land somewhere else. It was when the noise stopped that you were in trouble because it only took seconds for them to plummet from the sky, leaving you with no time to seek cover. Even if you found shelter, it rarely did much good.

Given the constant threat of bombings, and the inability to predict where and when Hitler might send his new bombs, sleeping in his own private bomb shelter seemed to Heinrich to be the soundest solution to staying alive. So, he set up house in the bomb shelter, despite the fact that it put him in close proximity to Rachel's neighbors.

His life was, if not comfortable, at least bearable. He had a secure location, an army cot for a bed, and warm weather. He had used up the ration cards that Rachel left for him, but he was still eating well, or well as could be expected in London. Between the food that "fell off the truck" when he was working with Jack and his illicit harvesting of unguarded "victory" gardens, he managed to feed himself. He knew, however, that this bounty wouldn't last. Come winter, if they were still at war, he would once again be reduced to climbing through rubbish bins in search of food, but for now, he was living quite well. The only things that troubled him were the doodlebugs and the loneliness. He missed Rachel. He dreamed about her when he slept, worried about her when he was awake, and in between he prayed that the war would end soon.

CHAPTER 42

THE DISCOVERY

December 22

I was cold, tired, and discouraged. The December sun gave off a weak watery light in a gray, colorless sky as Simon and I trudged along the streets, peering over fences and knocking on doors. Simon was annoyingly cheery and energetic.

We had worked our way down the list of addresses, but had only managed to confirm the location of one bomb shelter, which, according to the woman with whom I had just finished speaking, had been deemed a hazard and filled in three years ago. Discouraged, I clomped down the front steps. I had been so excited when Simon and I started our search, but now I was feeling depressed. It wasn't as if I thought it was going to be easy, I just didn't think it was going to be this hard. We had spent four hours traipsing around London, and we had nothing to show for our efforts.

Simon stood on the sidewalk waiting for me as I closed the front gate.

"This isn't working," I complained.

"What do you mean it isn't working? We've crossed off"—Simon looked down, consulting our list—"forty-three addresses."

I snorted. "Forty-three. That's nothing. Look at this list," I said, waving the paper at him. "My dad was right. This was a stupid idea. It'll take us years to check every possible building in London."

The corners of Simon's mouth turned up. Two dimples appeared like twin crescents as he grinned cheerfully at me. Usually I swooned at the sight of those dimples, but not now. Now I was cranky and they annoyed me.

"Why are you smiling?" I asked.

His grin widened.

"What's so funny?"

He grabbed me and pulled me close, planting a sloppy kiss on my lips. "You are adorable when you've got the hump."

I pulled back, put my hands on my hips, and stared up at him, eyes narrowed. "I've got the what?"

He studied me, his eyes glinting with mischief. "Yes. The hump. And you most definitely have got the hump."

I glared at him. I'd been living off and on in England for six months and I thought I had become familiar with British English. I was well versed in sayings like "Bob's your uncle" and "cheesed off." I knew that being "chuffed to bits" meant you were happy about something. I also knew the difference between a "tosser," a "wazzock," and a "wally," but I had never heard the expression "got the hump" before. I had a pretty good idea what it meant, given the context, but I wasn't one hundred percent sure. I suspected Simon had used it on purpose to prod me out of my bad mood.

"All right, Simon Fitzgibbon. You might as well tell me what it means."

"I'm not sure that's a good idea at the moment, given the look on your face," he countered.

"If you don't tell me, you're going to be the one with the hump. Right between your eyes," I warned.

He threw his head back and laughed.

Simon has this rumbling, deep-throated laugh that is almost impossible to resist. This time was no exception. I found myself grinning despite my best efforts.

The tiny lines in the corners of his eyes deepened. "It means that you are annoyed. Bothered, irritated, cheesed off, upset, unhappy, in a foul mood, feeling …"

"Okay. Okay." I held up my hands in surrender. "I get it. And you're right. I've definitely got the hump."

"No doubt about that," he agreed.

"So, what should we do about it?"

"Take a break?" Simon suggested.

I nodded. "That is a good idea. Maybe we can see if we can come up with a better plan. Besides, I think I need something to eat and drink."

"I won't say no to that."

We found a sandwich shop within walking distance and headed toward it. We hadn't been walking for very long, when my phone rang. Surprised, I answered it.

"Lily Deene?" a male voice asked.

"Yes."

"This is Inspector Shah. Is this a good time to speak with you?"

"Uhm. Yeah. Sure."

Simon watched me. One eyebrow raised inquiringly.

"Inspector Shah," I mouthed.

Inspector Shah continued speaking over the phone. "We've discovered something. I was wondering if you would be willing to have a look."

My heart rate bumped up a notch. "Harry? Did you find Harry?" I asked.

"We have found something of interest," he answered slowly. "I believe we have identified the location where you were being held captive."

"You found the bomb shelter?"

"We believe so. The lab technicians are almost finished. I thought that you might want to have a look. To confirm that this is the location. If you are feeling up to it."

"Just a minute," I said. I held the phone away from my mouth. "They think they found the bomb shelter," I told Simon. "They want to know if I can come look at it."

"Where is it?" he asked.

"Where is it?" I repeated into the phone.

Inspector Shah recited the address for me. I repeated it to Simon.

Simon entered the address into his phone and looked at the map. "That's not far from here. Tell him we can be there in half an hour."

Feelings of anticipation and dread corkscrewed in my stomach, leaving me feeling slightly sick as we exited the Tube station. I wasn't sure if I was ready to face seeing the bomb shelter. Not to mention, I was more than a little worried about how I would react. After all, I had fallen apart walking into my own bedroom, so I had no idea what would happen when I walked into the place where Harry and I had been held captive. I told myself that I would be okay. I wouldn't be walking in there alone. Simon and the police inspector would be with me, but I still couldn't shake the feeling of dread that settled in the pit of my stomach.

I must have looked a little stressed because Simon gave me a concerned look and asked if I was all right.

"I'm good," I told him with more confidence than I felt.

"We cross here," he said, gesturing to his left. "Are you sure that you want to do this?"

I nodded. "Maybe it will help me remember something that will help them find Harry," I said.

"If you change your mind, let me know. There's no shame in that. We'll just turn around and leave."

I gave him a tight little smile. "I know. Thanks."

"This is the street."

We turned onto the street and began walking along the sidewalk scanning the addresses of the buildings. The street was a mixture of old and new buildings. Older brick terraced homes giving way to larger, newer office and apartment buildings.

I looked up at the number of the closest building and made a quick calculation. "I think it might be over there, near the construction site," I said, pointing to the property surrounded by a chain-link fence.

We walked over to it.

Simon eyed the number of the building next door. "You're right. This has to be it."

A chain-link fence surrounded the entire lot. A padlocked gate, big enough for a truck to drive through, secured the site from trespassers. Simon and I walked up to the fence and peered between the chain links. There wasn't much to see. An empty bulldozer and a dump truck were parked next to a pile of rubble made up of broken boards and bricks and a half-demolished building. There was no sign of any human activity.

"I don't see anybody," I said.

The police must be around here somewhere," Simon commented, pointing to the police van parked on the street. "Why don't you call the inspector and tell him that we're here?"

I hit redial on my phone and waited for it to ring. When Inspector Shah picked up, I told him where we were.

"He's on his way," I told Simon. "We're to sit tight until he gets here."

Pangs of anxiety once again started fluttering in my stomach. I looked through the opening in the fence and stared at what was left of the building, searching for something that might resemble a bomb shelter. "What do you think this building was?" I asked Simon.

"I don't know, but there is a sign on the side of the fence over there. It might tell us something. We can have a look if you like."

"We might as well."

We walked along the fence to the sign. In bold black lettering, it read: Coming Soon: Business Offices for Orlav Vodka Products, Intl.

I stared at the sign for a moment, not quite able to process what I was reading. I read the words again: Orlav Vodka Products. I knew that name. Why? Then it came to me in a sudden flash of memory, my dad talking about his business deal with the Russian vodka company.

I stared at the sign, my eyes glued to the words as my fragile outward shell of calm became shot through with little cracks. Orlav Vodka Products. I was almost positive it was the company that my dad had mentioned to me, but I didn't know what that meant. There couldn't be two companies in London with the same name. Not that name.

My dad's business partners owned this building. My dad knew the people who owned this building. The building where I had been taken after I'd been kidnapped. Why would the kidnappers choose to hide me in a building owned by my dad's business partners? It couldn't be a coincidence, but if it wasn't a coincidence, then that would mean that my dad was somehow involved with my kidnapping. That didn't make any sense either. Thoughts spun around inside my head in a kind of whirlpool. I couldn't seem to make the pieces fit together.

"I have to go," I told Simon abruptly.

"All right. Let's go."

"No. I need to go. I need to … I need to see my dad."

Simon's eyebrows shot up to his hairline. "You're dad? You want to see your dad? Now?"

I nodded.

"All right, then. If that's what you want. We'll go find

your dad. Just call the inspector first, to let him know that we can't meet him."

"No. I need to go alone."

A faint worry line appeared between his eyebrows. "I don't understand."

"I need to go alone. You stay here and meet Inspector Shah."

"Why?"

"I just need to see my dad, that's all. I'll, uhm. I've got to go."

I turned to go, but Simon placed a hand on my sleeve.

"Lily, are you all right?" he asked, his expression troubled.

I gave my arm an impatient tug. "I have to go," I told him.

"Lily, at least let me walk you to …"

"No!" I said more loudly than I intended. "No," I repeated more calmly. "I need to go by myself. I'll be fine. I need to talk to my dad about something." I stared up at him, hoping he would understand.

"All right then. If you're sure."

"I am."

"Do you want me to wait for you?" he asked simply.

I gave my head an impatient shake. "I don't know how long I'll be. I'll meet you back at the flat." I opened my bag, took out the apartment keys, and handed them to him.

"All right. I'll wait for you at the flat then."

I turned and began walking briskly toward the Tube station. I could feel Simon's troubled gaze following me.

CHAPTER 43

FINDING HARRY

December 22

Simon stood and watched her walk away, feeling a bit stunned. He had expected that coming here would be difficult for her, but he hadn't expected this. He still wasn't sure what just happened. Was she having another anxiety attack? He didn't think so. She didn't seem to be frightened, just, he paused, searching for a word to describe her state of mind, finally settling on the word agitated. She was agitated. Something about the sign had upset her.

He turned to read the sign again. He shook his head as he stared at it feeling puzzled. Perhaps he was wrong. Perhaps her reaction had nothing to do with the sign. Quite possibly, she was just feeling nervous about meeting with the police inspector, but if that was the case, why the sudden need to see her dad?

He turned and watched as she disappeared around the

corner. Should he follow her? She wouldn't be pleased if she found him out. He wavered for a moment. Finally deciding that given her present emotional state, it would be better to risk a row than to have something happen to her.

His moment of indecisiveness cost him. He had waited too long. He saw her enter the Tube station, but he lost her underground. He hadn't been quick enough, and she boarded a train before he could get down to the platform.

Now what? he thought, as the train disappeared into the tunnel. Now nothing. There was nothing more he could do for her. He had no idea where her father was staying, nor did he have any means of contacting him. He could only hope that Lily was going to be all right. Glumly, he climbed up the steps and walked back toward the construction site. If nothing else, the inspector might be able to give him an update on their investigation.

Inspector Shah was waiting in front of the padlocked gate.

"Mr. Fitzgibbon," he said. "Is Ms. Deene with you?"

Simon shook his head. "You just missed her. She wasn't feeling well."

The inspector looked sympathetic. "Ah. I see. That is too bad. Well, since we are both here, perhaps you would be interested in having a look. I think there is something you should see."

Simon nodded.

The inspector unlocked the padlock and opened the gate. "This way," he said. "Mind your step."

Simon followed the inspector to the back of a partially demolished building.

"Careful, please," Shah said, stepping around the debris. "It's just over here."

The inspector led him to a span of recently exposed earth.

"When the construction workers cleared away the vegetation, they came upon this," Shah said, pointing to a rectangular opening level with the ground as if a trap door had once been there. A heavy metal sheet large enough to cover the opening lay on the ground next to it. The entire area had been marked off with stakes and police tape.

As Simon watched, the head and shoulders of a technician dressed in white coveralls appeared to rise from the hole in the ground. The technician nodded to Inspector Shah when he caught sight of them.

"Is your crew finished with this lot?" Shah asked.

"Yes. That's the last of it for now. Waiting for the ME to give us the go for the rest."

"Good. Then we'll just pop down for a quick look. If that's all right?"

The technician shrugged. "Fine by me."

Inspector Shah lifted the crime scene tape for the technician to duck under it, then motioned for Simon to do the same.

"We think this might have been an old root cellar for the original house," the inspector explained. "The original building on this site dates back to Victorian times. You can see the old brickwork on the stairs." He gestured to the walls bordering the steps with a flick of his wrist.

Simon peered into the opening. The inspector was right. The walls were made of cement and old bricks. A set of steps descended underground to a small landing where a thick wooden door stood ajar.

Simon followed down the narrow steps, pausing halfway down to allow the inspector to open the door wider because there wasn't enough room on the small landing for the two of them. Shah stepped inside the cellar and waited for Simon to join him.

The room was small. The floors and walls were built with the same combination of brick and cement that had been on the stairwell, the ceiling was brick interspersed with wooden beams. Even with the door wide open, it was very dark. It didn't appear that there were any windows or other openings inside the small room. He thought he could just make out what looked like a low wooden shelf along the far side of the room.

"No electric lights, I'm afraid," the inspector said. He removed a torch from his pocket and flicked it on, sweeping the beam of light around the room.

One part of the room had collapsed. A pile of rubble and broken bricks lay in a large mound.

"Looks like there was a bit of a cave-in," Simon said as the light from Shah's torch illuminated the rubble.

"Yes. Our techs think that it happened during the war. World War II," he explained, sweeping his torch across the rubble. "Most likely the same German bomb that damaged the original building caused this. The original house was damaged and rebuilt sometime after the war. We think that the new owners didn't realize that the cellar was here when they built on this site."

"So, this was used as a bomb shelter during the war?"

"Looks like it. We found remnants of wooden frames and canvas material from what might have been a government-issued army cot. That would be consistent with the same time period."

The light from Shah's torch swung around the room, coming to rest on a white plastic ice chest.

"This is what tipped off the construction crew. They uncovered this opening when they started the demolition and decided to have a quick look around. When they saw the ice chest, they were worried that it might be someone's squat. They did a bit of exploring in order to make sure no one was down here before they started the demolition."

Simon wrinkled his forehead perplexed. "But if they thought it was someone's squat, why did they ring you?"

"Ah. That," Inspector Shah said. "They didn't actually call me. They put a call through to the local station. A colleague of mine contacted me when the phone call came in because he knew I was looking for a bomb shelter."

"Right, but I still don't understand. Why ring the police at all? If someone was squatting here, they just needed to make sure it was empty before finishing up with the demo.

Right? As long as the place was empty, they wouldn't need to ring anyone."

"Correct," Shah agreed. "However, they made an additional discovery, which is the reason I suggested you and Lily come and have a look." Shah flicked his torch beam up and swept it along the back wall. "The construction crew called the police because they found this," he said, his light coming to rest on a human skull.

Simon stood riveted by the sight of the skull among the debris. "A skeleton?" he asked immediately, feeling stupid for doing so. Obviously, it was a skeleton.

Shah nodded. "Our techs are fairly certain he's been down here since the war. Probably died in the blitz. We're not sure if he was killed when the bomb hit, or if the poor sod ended up being entombed in the shelter that was supposed to protect him. The ME will have a look and we might get lucky and be able to identify him.

"The bones are old, but the crew who found him didn't know that. They saw the skull and closed down work for the day."

"You wanted to show Lily the skeleton? Why?"

"I'm fairly certain that this was where they kept Lily. It fits her description of the place. Though we'll have to wait for the forensics lab to confirm," he added. "You know that Lily has been very insistent that we continue our search for her missing companion Harry?"

Simon nodded.

He moved his torch around the room. "As you can see, there are no other doors, windows, vents, or alcoves. Unless Harry was in this very room with her, she would not have been able to communicate with him. Yet, she insists that he was not in this room with her. That he was in some other location."

"Let me show you something." He closed the door behind them and turned off his torch. A dense impenetrable blackness engulfed them.

The inspector was standing next to Simon, but with the

door closed, the darkness was so complete he could no longer see him.

"Sometimes a mind under great stress may develop delusions as a means of coping with the stress. I'm certain that you're familiar with stories of people crossing the desert hallucinating about water."

"Yes," Simon replied.

"Lily was abducted, drugged, and locked in this dark room alone. That is what I believe will be confirmed by our forensics team. I suspect the person or people who brought her here also covered the opening at the top of the stairs with the metal sheet you saw lying on the ground. This room would have been even darker and more claustrophobic. She must have been terrified." Inspector Shah's torch flicked on, once again illuminating the skull. "I believe her mind supplied her with what she most needed while she was here, trapped and alone in the dark, a companion. Someone to comfort her in her distress."

As Simon stared at the gleaming skull, he felt a sharp frisson of electricity shoot up his spine, causing the back of his skull to prickle unpleasantly.

Inspector Shah opened the door, and the oppressive darkness receded. He turned off his torch and looked over at Simon. "I believe that this skeleton is her companion Harry."

Simon stared at the skull. The inspector was right. He was sure that the skeleton was Harry, but he wasn't so sure that Harry was a figment of Lily's imagination.

Shah's light shifted as it moved across the brick walls, illuminating something beside the skull. Simon noticed a faint but very recognizable heart drawn on the uneven surface of the bricks. A heart inscribed with the letters R and H.

CHAPTER 44

A FATHER AND A DAUGHTER

December 22

I called my father and told him that I needed to see him. I think he could tell by the sound of my voice that something was wrong. He gave me the address of his hotel and told me that he would be waiting for me. I grabbed the first train traveling in the right direction.

My anxiety had disappeared, replaced by confusion. During the train ride to my dad's hotel, I tried to quiet the three little words spinning around and around inside my head: Orlav Vodka Products.

There are more than seven million people living in London and hundreds of thousands of buildings. The chance of my kidnapper coincidently choosing a building owned by my father's business partners was almost non-existent, but if it wasn't a coincidence, that would mean my father … I pushed the thought away. I didn't want to think about that, not until I had spoken to him.

I got off at London Victoria Station. As usual, it was a total zoo. The platforms were jammed with tourists hoping to get a glimpse of the royals and Londoners hoping to finish their last-minute Christmas shopping. I fought my way through the crush of humanity to the street and walked to the Goring Hotel.

The Goring is one of the oldest luxury hotels in London. Named after its founder, Otto Goring, it is famous because it is located at Beeston Place, which means it is next-door neighbor to Buckingham Palace. Yes, that would be *the* Buckingham Palace, home to the British royal family. The fact that my father was staying at the Goring didn't really surprise me. My dad likes to live as if he is wealthy, unfortunately for him, he isn't.

The hotel was decorated for Christmas. Flocked holly wreaths and swag festooned the outside. The twinkling lights of a decorated tree shone through the front window. It was beautiful, but I barely even noticed. I was not feeling the holiday spirit.

I walked up the red-carpeted stairs to the front doors where I was ushered inside by a very proper English doorman wearing a black bowler, yellow scarf, its matching handkerchief peeking out of his breast pocket of his blazer in a perfectly folded triangle.

"Good afternoon, Miss," he said, opening the door.

Inside, two footmen in red tailcoats and black vests with gold buttons greeted me a second time. I stood inside, looking uncertainly around the well-appointed lobby for my father.

He wasn't hard to spot. He stuck out like a sore thumb among the British and European guests in the lobby. He was chatting with the woman at the reception desk. Tan and fit, wearing khaki pants, an open-collared white shirt, and blue blazer, he looked like he had just stepped out of the clubhouse at a Southern Californian golf resort.

He caught sight of me, said something that made the woman behind the counter laugh, before turning toward me. "Tiger Lily," he said, striding across the lobby, his arms open.

"Hi, Dad."

My dad's eyebrows rose at my subdued greeting. "Hmm. You've got a serious look on your face. What's going on?"

"Is there someplace private where we can talk?"

"Oh, my. This must be something serious," he said lightly. "Hmm." He looked around. "Why don't we go into the bar?" he asked, gesturing to his left. "I'm sure we can find a quiet table."

He ushered me through the doors to a corner table. It was a gray and gloomy afternoon, but a cheerful fire crackled in the fireplace. We sat across from each other in the deep, soft leather chairs. Any other time, I would have enjoyed the ambiance, but right now, my stomach churned anxiously.

"So," my father said, looking at me expectantly. "What is so urgent that you had to travel across London to talk to me today?"

I hesitated for a moment, trying to decide the best way to ask him. "Inspector Shah called. They think they found the bomb shelter."

"Bomb shelter?"

"The place where I was held after I was, uhm taken," I told him.

"Really?"

"They have to confirm it, but he's pretty sure."

"Well, that is good news," my dad said, his voice full of false cheer. "It looks like I'll have to change my opinion of the London police force and give credit where credit is due."

At that moment, I think I knew. It was something about the way he said it. I'd heard that same hollow laugh enough times to know he was hiding something.

"It's kind of funny, Dad. It was one of the addresses you were going to look at after your business meeting."

"Well, I am sorry about that, Lily. I was going to call you. My meeting took longer than I anticipated, and I didn't get around to it. I was going to try and get to it today. I guess the inspector saved me a trip."

I didn't say anything.

"You know," he continued. "It's actually a good thing that you called me today. Things have changed, and I am leaving London earlier than I had planned."

"So, your business deal is finished?" I asked.

"Yes. We wrapped things up yesterday, in fact."

"You got the contract?"

He flashed me a wide smile, his teeth gleaming very white against his tan skin. "Yes. I was a little worried at the beginning, but everything has worked out."

I didn't want to hear the answer to my next question, but I couldn't stop myself from asking. "I'm trying to remember. What was the name of the company again?" I asked, a hard lump settling in the pit of my stomach.

"It's not a company you would know," my dad said smoothly.

"Didn't you tell me that the company was Russian?"

His eyes skittered away from me. He glanced around the room briefly before returning my gaze. "Did I? I don't remember."

"Funny. The company that owned the construction site where they found the bomb shelter is also Russian."

"Really? That is interesting."

"The name of the company was Orlav Vodka Products." I locked my eyes onto his. "Isn't that name of the company you've been working with?"

He froze, just for a millisecond, then quickly recovered. The hearty laugh and wide smile were back, although he couldn't quite hide the flicker of fear I saw in his eyes. "You've got a good memory, Tiger Lily. You must get that from your mother."

I said nothing and waited. Until that moment, I had been hoping that I was wrong, that I had somehow misunderstood. I stared at him, silently daring him to explain, to tell me that he had nothing to do with my kidnapping. Maybe I should have asked him directly, but then if I had, and he had told me that he wasn't, I wasn't sure I would believe him.

He stretched his arm toward me, as if he was going to touch me, but then thinking better of it, curled his fingers into his palm and brought his hand up to cover his mouth as he gave a little cough and cleared his throat. He gazed at me, his eyes tinged with sadness.

"Life doesn't always go the way you plan, Lily. You work hard and do the best you can, but then one day you find yourself in an impossible situation. You realize it doesn't matter how hard you've worked. You are going to fail. When you reach that point, you have to make a decision. You can either do what needs to be done or lose everything you've worked for your entire life."

"You did this to me." My voice shook. "You had your own daughter kidnapped. For what? Money?"

"No," he said quickly. "That wasn't the plan."

"Don't!" My voice rose. "Don't lie to me."

He stood abruptly. "Lily, I had no choice, but I would never knowingly let anyone hurt you."

I stared at him so overcome with emotion that I couldn't even speak.

"I would never have let them hurt you," he repeated. "It's the truth. You need to believe that."

I stared up at him silently and accusingly.

He bent down and kissed my cheek lightly. "Bye, Tiger Lily."

I watched him go, the truth leaking into me like acid. My dad had used me to get money. My dad or someone he knew, drugged me, kidnapped me, and locked me in a bomb shelter for money.

In a daze, I stood and left the hotel, though I have no recollection of doing so. I wandered around London. I walked through the city completely unaware of my surroundings, my emotions alternating between grief, anger, hurt, and betrayal. I knew I had a decision to make, but it was too much to take in all at once. I was numb. As much as I wanted to deny everything, I couldn't. But that didn't mean I was ready to accept it either. My own father had kidnapped me or had me kidnapped. Why? Why would he do something like that? He didn't love me. He used me to get money. There was no excuse for what he did. There was nothing that he could say that could possibly justify what he did. I was heartbroken.

My dad had said that he had chosen to do what needed to be done so that he didn't lose everything. I now knew that I wasn't included in his definition of everything, because he had lost me. Forever.

By the time I arrived back at the flat, it was dark. Simon opened the door before I finished knocking. A look of profound relief crossed his face when he saw me. He gathered me into his arms and pulled me tightly against him. I leaned into the warmth of him as he held me close and I let his quiet, steady strength fill up the empty place in my broken heart.

He took a half step back and gazed at me, a jumble of emotions in his eyes. His voice was quiet, but I could tell he was working hard to keep his temper under control. "Don't ever do that to me again. I had no idea where you were or what had happened to you. I was half out of my mind with worry."

I tilted my head and looked up at him. I felt horrible. I had completely forgotten about Simon. He had tried to ring me several times, but I hadn't been ready to talk to anyone, not even Simon, so I turned off my phone. He must have been crazy with worry when he couldn't get in touch with me. "I'm sorry," I told him. "I wasn't thinking."

The muscle in his jaw jumped and he exhaled forcefully. "No, you weren't. Another half hour and I was going to call the police. You should have let me know you were all right."

I laid a hand on his arm. "I know. I'm really sorry that I made you worry. I had a lot to think about and I just couldn't face anyone." Just saying that made my throat squeeze tight and before I could stop myself, I was crying.

Almost immediately the anger drained out of him. "Do you want to talk about it?"

I shook my head.

"Have you eaten?"

"No." I sniffled.

"I'll boil some pasta."

My sleepless night, not to mention the emotional rollercoaster I'd been riding, finally caught up with me. By the time I'd finished the pasta, I could barely keep my eyes open. Simon tenderly tucked me in before clearing the dishes. The second my head hit the pillow, I fell into a deep dreamless sleep.

In the morning, I told Simon about my father. Simon listened intently, his expression grim.

Part of me wanted Simon to say that it would be all right if I did nothing. I think I was hoping that maybe, if I didn't do anything or say anything, it would make it less real and I could pretend that my father hadn't done anything bad. I was torn between wanting to do the right thing for Sir Richard and wanting to protect my father, because despite everything he'd done, he was still my father and I loved him.

"I know you want to protect him, but the truth is, he has hurt a lot of people. Not just you. It is not your job to protect him. You are not responsible for your father. You really don't owe him anything, but you have to do what is right for you. I won't say anything if you don't want me to, but you need to be sure that this is a secret you can live with for the rest of your life."

Of course, Simon was right. Keeping this secret would make me just like my father. I couldn't protect him without hurting myself, my mom, and Sir Richard.

"I know I need to call Sir Richard and my mom, but I just don't know how. I don't know what to say."

"Perhaps this isn't something you can tell them over the phone," Simon said simply.

CHAPTER 45

THE LONG AND THE SHORT OF THINGS

Four Months Later

Simon and I drove back to Brynmoor Manor. That same afternoon I told everything to my mom and Sir Richard. My father ended up taking a plea bargain with the police. Here is what I managed to piece together from my dad's testimony and the police investigation. My dad's business partners turned out to be involved with the Russian mafia. I guess my dad promised to help them funnel money into the United States as part of a money-laundering scheme by setting up distribution through the vodka company. It didn't work out and my dad ended up owing the Russians a lot of money.

According to my dad, the kidnapping was the Russians' idea. Apparently, the Russian mafia has a lot of experience extorting ransom from wealthy people. The police said that the Russians often use their ties to local criminal gangs to kidnap or blackmail people outside of Russia. My dad still insists that he didn't know that they were going to kidnap me. He says that he thought they were going to steal art and valuables from Sir Richard's apartment. Of course, he also said that they promised him my "kidnapping" was going to involve sticking me in a hotel room and leaving me to watch television until the ransom was paid. Obviously, that wasn't what happened. It's hard to know how much of what my dad told me is true. I'm not sure I believe him when he says he didn't know anything about my kidnapping, but I am trying to. Why? I guess because I don't want my memories of my father to be nothing more than lies. If I thought that he had planned my kidnapping, then everything about my relationship with him would be a lie, and I am not ready to face that. It's easier to believe that he is what he has always been, a charming scoundrel, only this time he got in over his head.

And Harry? Simon told me about Harry. I think at some level, I knew what he was going to tell me. Perhaps, I had always known the truth about Harry.

Finding Harry's skeleton only confirmed Inspector Shah's belief that Harry was nothing more than a figment of my imagination, something I invented to cope with the trauma of my abduction. My mother, Sir Richard, and the doctors all believe it, too, but I know they are wrong. Harry was there in the bomb shelter, with me.

I truly believe that there are times when the dead stay with us, tethered to this world by some kind of unfinished business. Perhaps, there is someone they need to help, or a wrong they need to right, or simply an emotion that ties them to a particular place. Whatever it is, they aren't ready to leave this world and so they stay behind. I believe that Harry was here on Earth because there was something he needed to do. I don't doubt that for a second. Unfortunately, I probably won't ever know what it was that was keeping Harry tied to this world.

I had wanted to see Harry again, if only to thank him

and say goodbye, but I wasn't able to. Inspector Shah called a few days after I returned to Brynmoor Manor to tell me that the Medical Examiner had removed Harry and sealed the site. I guess a tourist accidentally fell into the bomb shelter and they had to close it. After Harry was removed, the police gave permission to the construction crew to finish their demolition.

Perhaps Harry just wanted to be found. I hope so. I know that Harry wasn't a hallucination. He saved me, and for that I will always be grateful to him.

Me? All in all, I'm doing pretty well. I still feel uncomfortable in small, enclosed spaces, but the panic attacks have disappeared. My insomnia and nightmares are gone, too. I am back at Kings Cross College and living in student housing.

CHAPTER 46

THE END OF THE STORY

The Daily Telegraph

SECOND BODY FOUND IN CELLAR

In a macabre twist of fate, a construction crew discovered a second body in an underground cellar where a skeleton had been recovered several days prior. The cellar originally part of a Victorian estate had been used as a bomb shelter during World War II.

Forensic experts earlier identified the skeleton as that of a young male who appeared to have been killed in a German bombing raid during the Second World War. The discovery of the second body, identified as Miss Rachel Cohen of Oxfordshire, age 96, occurred two days after this journal published reports of the skeleton's location.

Miss Cohen's niece, Mrs. Susan Miller, could not explain how her aunt came to be at 2765 Crouch Way.

According to Mrs. Miller, Miss Cohen had asked if she would drive her to London to see an old friend. Because of her poor health, Mrs. Miller suggested that her aunt stay overnight in a hotel and offered to fetch her the following day.

"I offered to drive her to meet her friend, but she told me not to bother. She said that her friend was waiting for her and she would take a taxi," Mrs. Miller stated.

Miss Cohen's friend has yet to be identified. Police believe that Ms. Cohen became lost or disoriented and wandered into the construction site by mistake through a gate that had been left unlocked. It appears that Ms. Cohen died of natural causes. However, an investigation into her cause of death is currently pending.

FALL IN LOVE WITH LILY'S ADVENTURES

Lily Deene has a new dream guy. There's just one small problem. He's dead.

Seventeen-year-old Lily Deene has no choice but to spend her summer at Brynmoor Manor in England where there are more sheep than people. She isn't thrilled, but after her mother enlists Simon, the housekeeper's son, to give her horseback riding lessons, Lily decides to make the best of a bad situation. It turns out that it's not all tea and crumpets at the manor house. Long buried secrets are stirring. Secrets that are haunting her dreams and Lily quickly finds herself galloping straight into danger.

Excerpt:

As my eyes adjusted, I could see the vague outline of something lying on the ground. I struggled to make out what it was. At first, I thought a tree had fallen or been cut and left in the middle of the pasture. I stared at the shape, trying to figure out why it was there.

Suddenly, I felt my blood drain away in fear. I opened my mouth to scream, but there was no sound. My breath caught in my throat. It wasn't a log at all! It was the body of a man! I stared in horror at the still figure lying on the ground.

I stood unable to move for several seconds. His body lay so still. I was afraid he might be dead. I forced my shaking legs to move forward. As I did so I became aware that I was not alone. I could sense the presence of someone else nearby, hidden in the mist.

"Whose there?" I called out, my voice trembling with fear.

Silence. I stood still and tilted my head, listening. The hair on the back of my neck prickled. I heard a sound and whipped around frantically trying to locate the origin of the noise. A flash of movement caught my eye and I watched as a ghostly apparition disappeared into the mist.

With one ghost on her mind, and another haunting

it, Lily's been ghosted...literally.

Hoping to rekindle her romance with Simon, Lily Deene travels to Anchoret House in the remote Scottish Highlands. Despite a warning to beware of spirits wandering the moors, Lily is drawn to investigate the mysterious death of a young bride, Mairi Morris. She soon realizes that death haunts Anchoret House, and that she too may be in danger.

Lily Deene barely escaped with her life during her last encounter with a ghost, now she's facing another dangerous spirit. If you love mysteries with a little piece of history, you'll love the Lily Deene Series.

Excerpt:

I studied the stonework below Mairi's portrait while he spoke. It was strange, but even I could see that the workmanship was not of the same quality as the rest of the walls in the room. The stones were rougher and not as uniform in shape and color. I reached out to touch one of the stones.

As soon as my hand touched the cold, rough surface, I felt a sudden surge, like the shock from an electrical current charge through my body. It rushed through me, leaving me feeling as raw and exposed as if I had lost a layer of skin. My heart slammed into my chest and the room around me suddenly vanished. I saw nothing but darkness, so black and impenetrable it was like a solid wall. Pain! Sorrow! Rage! Emotions jolted through me, shuddering up my spine and exploding inside my head. I think I grabbed my head with both my hands, but I'm not sure. The only thing I was aware of was the pain as the dark pressed against me, stealing my breath away.

Strangled choked sounds creaked out of my throat. I couldn't talk. I couldn't move. I was like one of the children in Ben's story about the kelpie unable to free myself. Some part of my brain knew I was being dragged down deeper and deeper into the icy black water, but I could do nothing about it. All I knew was pain. Deep, raw pain. I forgot where I was. I forgot who I was. I had no sense of anything except that I was drowning in pain.

AVAILABLE WHERE BOOKS ARE SOLD….

ACKNOWLEDGEMENTS

Special thanks to Wendy Blubaugh for generously sharing her expertise and her daughter (Emily you are an awesome cover girl!). Our website is beautiful because of you.

Barbara Ness and Joe Weinzettle, were early and enthusiastic readers of the original draft. We are grateful to Mike "Eagle Eye" McDermott, every writer should have a friend who is a librarian.

Kim Hobin, Corey Meitchik, and Steve Salm also deserve to be mentioned for helping Rachel be wise in words as well as deeds.

InkSpell Publishers who believed in the Lily Deene books and our editor Yezanira Venecia who makes our stories shine.

A heartfelt thank you to a wonderful father-in-law and grandpa Jim "Chook" Weinzettle for sharing his stories of WW2.

Finally, John and Cristobal, you are the wind beneath our wings.

ABOUT THE AUTHOR

(photo from 2004)

Annie Grace Roberts is a mother-daughter writing team from California. They share a love of adventure and happy endings. Neither has ever met a ghost they didn't like.

www. AnnieGraceRoberts.com
AnnieGracebooks@gmail.com
AGRoberts_books twitter
AnnieGraceRoberts instagram
facebook: /www.facebook.com/Annie-Grace-Roberts

www.ingramcontent.com/pod-product-compliance
Lightning Source LLC
LaVergne TN
LVHW091123080826
845145LV00008B/2022